To Ja...

The
Man in The
Skirt

Best Wishes

G Walsh

This book is dedicated to someone very special. This book is dedicated to…
YOU!

The Fearless Four
Book One:

The
Man in The
Skirt

by
Gez Walsh

The King's England Press
1998

ISBN 1 872438 25 3

The Man in The Skirt is typeset by Moose Manuscripts in
Perpetua 12pt and published by
The King's England Press,
21 Commercial Road, Goldthorpe
Rotherham, South Yorkshire, S63 9BL.

Second Impression, 2000

Printed and bound in Great Britain by
Woolnough Bookbinding
Irthlingborough
Northamptonshire.

Foreword

Many years ago, when I was just a young pup, my grandfather told my brother John and myself wonderful stories of how he and his cousin Kelly fought against banshees and other strange creatures. This was the inspiration for *The Man in The Skirt*.

After visiting many schools all over the country reading from my poetry books (I might have visited yours - I'm the tall, ugly bloke who got the teachers up dancing) I collected information from children as to what they would like to read in a story. So this story contains all the ingredients that they asked for: horror, comedy, adventure, tough girls, stupid boys and farts.

The story starts when Wilf Sexton swallows a small stone when he's messing around in a museum. From then on, nothing else will ever be the same for Wilf. He learns that not all people are who they claim to be. He can trust no one. Someone wants him dead - but who?

This book is just the start of a long journey for Wilf and his three friends Burp, Molly and Kirsty.

So, travel with them through the laughs, tears, twists and turns. And remember - trust no one!

Part One

The Stone Thingy

"Come along, children," said Miss Dennis, the teacher of class six. "Now, these are objects of Celtic art."

In front of the children was a large table covered with a green baize cloth. On the table were various objects ranging from a bronze shield, with a black serpent engraved round the edge, to an earthenware jug which had been pieced together like some crude jigsaw.

The children looked on, very bored, as Miss Dennis explained to them just how the objects were made and where they had come from.

Standing at the back of the group was Wilf Sexton and his best friend, Burp Dawson. These two lads were the sort of people who could get themselves into trouble when they were asleep. They always messed about, instead of listening to what they were being told, and today was no different.

Burp, who had got his nickname because he could produce humungous burps at will, something that his friend Wilf had always admired, was at this moment curling back his eyelids because Wilf had challenged him to see who could pull the most disgusting face. He pushed his nose up so it looked like the snout of a pig and, putting his fingers in his mouth, spread his lips so they looked like a fish with a hook in its mouth.

Wilf, meanwhile, was trying to act like a gorilla and both lads were so busy messing about that they hadn't noticed the rest of the class had moved on to another part of the museum.

It was Wilf who first noticed that everyone had gone. He was stood with his legs bent, beating his chest, when he stopped and pointed to where the rest of the class had been standing.

"Ugh! Ugh!" he said in his best gorilla voice. Burp stopped and turned to look where Wilf was pointing. The lads looked at each other then burst out laughing.

"Come on Wilf, we'll have to go and find the rest of the class."

"No, let's stay here a bit," replied Wilf. "I'm fed up of looking at old pots, and besides, no one will notice we're missing." He walked over to the baize-covered table. "Just look at all this rubbish. I mean, it cost my mum five pounds for me to come on this school outing, and what for? If I'd wanted to look at a load of old pots I would have gone to my gran's, she has lots of them."

"It's better than doing maths."

"This is very true, young man, very true indeed," Wilf replied, a big grin on his face. He looked at the sign on the table which said "PLEASE DO NOT TOUCH THE EXHIBITS" and then picked up what looked like a stone bean engraved with strange patterns. Wilf put it close to his eye and stared.

"I mean, what the heck is this supposed to be?" he asked, holding it out in his palm.

"It looks like a well-baked bean to me, young man," laughed Burp.

Wilf and Burp always called each other young man when they messed around because Mr Thomas, their head teacher, always called them this whenever they were caught, which was quite often. He would boom in a loud, theatrical voice, "Once more you misbehave! Come here, young man." The boys thought this sounded hilarious.

Wilf looked at the stone thingy and shook his head. "I can't believe we've travelled all the way from Huddersfield to Manchester just to look at an old baked bean."

"But is it a tasty old baked bean?" asked Burp.

"I don't know, young man. I'll have a little taste and tell you," said Wilf, popping the stone thingy into his mouth.

"What on earth are you two doing here?" boomed a loud voice from behind them. Both boys froze with fright; it was the unmistakable voice of Mr Thomas. The lads turned to face him rather sheepishly.

He was a very large man, with a large red nose and a bald patch which he tried to hide by combing his hair from the sides over the top to cover it up. His suit looked two sizes too small, owing to the fact that it was about twenty years old. It was black and the elbows and knees had gone shiny, while the trousers were tight to his legs but flared out at the bottom. He pointed his huge, ape-like finger at the lads.

"Sexton, come here, young man!" he boomed, as if he was performing in a Shakespeare play. Wilf nervously walked over to the huge, ape-like man. Since he was only

11

small and rather skinny it made Mr Thomas appear to be twice the size he was.

"Now tell me, young man, why are you and Dawson messing about here while the rest of your class are away being educated?"

"W... we got lost, Sir," stuttered Wilf.

"Got lost? Got lost?" boomed Mr Thomas, just in case they hadn't heard him the first time. "How do you manage to lose a teacher and thirty children?"

Wilf was just about to give him a brilliant excuse he'd quickly thought up about how Burp had fainted, fallen into his arms and been given mouth-to-mouth resuscitation, when Mr Thomas cut in.

"Go forth and find your class, and report to me when you get back to school." This was just as well because Mr Thomas could spot a good lie a mile away, and Wilf's was not a good lie.

Both lads shuffled away with their heads held low, Burp trying hard to stifle his laughter, Wilf with a serious look on his face.

"When old Thomas has gone, we'll go and put the stone thingy back on the table," said Burp in a hushed voice.

"I can't!" whispered Wilf with a worried look.

"Don't be scared, he won't catch us."

"It's not that," said Wilf.

"Well what, then?" asked Burp looking puzzled. Wilf put his hand to his forehead and started tapping it like people do when they have just done something they wished they hadn't. He spoke slowly and quietly.

"You know when old Thomas shouted? Well, he made

12

me jump."

"He made me jump, too," said Burp looking even more puzzled.

"Yes, but you didn't swallow the stone thingy when you jumped, did you?" said Wilf, raising his voice. Burp burst out laughing.

"You mean you swallowed the two thousand-year-old bean?"

"Yes!" snapped Wilf, panic setting in. All he could think about was whether the bean had got stuck in his stomach - he might die! Or what if it carried a strange virus, one that no doctor alive had ever seen before that had no known cure. "Oh, what am I going to do?" cried Wilf, close to tears.

Burp could see that his friend was getting upset, so he tried to stop himself from laughing.

"Look Wilf, don't worry yourself. My little brother once swallowed a paper clip," he said in his best reassuring voice. Then he let out a big snort as a laugh burst out quite unexpectedly.

"What happened to him?" enquired Wilf with concern.

"Well, he had to have six major operations and part of his lower bowel removed," replied Burp, keeping his face as straight as he could.

"What?!" screamed Wilf. Burp put his hand over Wilf's mouth because he was starting to get very loud, and the last thing he wanted was for old Thomas to hear them.

"I'm only messing, Wilf. The doctor just told my mum to keep an eye on my brother's pooh, to make sure that the paper clip came back out."

"And did it?"

13

"Of course it did. Three days later my mum found two turds neatly clipped together in his potty." Burp fell about, hysterical with laughter.

"But I don't use a potty. How will I know if it's come back out?" said Wilf, shaking Burp by his arm in the hope that he would stop laughing. Burp calmed himself down a little.

"Look, stop worrying, it'll all come out in the wash," he said, then burst out in hysterical laughter again. Burp finally calmed down. "Come on, let's go and find the rest of our class before we get ourselves into any more trouble."

The two lads ran out of the room and up a large marble staircase which had pictures of long-dead people on each side. At the top of the stairs was a large, old grandfather clock which had an enormous pendulum swinging below it. Off to the right was a huge room filled with glass cases. In the reflection of these cases Wilf and Burp could see their class, still being bored by Miss Dennis, so they sneaked in and joined the back of the group.

Wilf had been right - no one had missed them at all.

Another half an hour or so was spent looking at old pots and pieces of stone.

"Right children, everyone back to the main entrance. I hope that today has given you some good ideas for your projects on the Celts. There's certainly been a lot for you to digest," said Miss Dennis.

"Some of us have digested more than others, eh Wilf?" said Burp, nudging his friend.

"Shut up, will you. I'll be glad when this thing comes back out."

"I've just had a thought, Wilf. What if you fart it out like a bullet?" said Burp, falling about laughing again until Wilf gave him a smack over the back of the head to make him shut up.

All the other children had gathered at the main entrance. Some were buying souvenirs from an old woman who worked in the museum shop.

"She looks older than that stone bean I swallowed," said Wilf, watching the old lady huff and puff as she tried to fathom out how to use the till.

15

Then Mr Thomas made his entrance, as he always did, thinking that he'd just walked on stage to take a curtain call in the West End. Mr Thomas, you see, was a frustrated actor. He had been performing amateur dramatics for the last thirty years and always believed that one day he would get his big break; the trouble was that it had got to the stage where he couldn't work out which was acting and which was real life.

"Right, children!" he boomed, with just a slight quake in his voice as though he was about to perform a death scene in a Shakespeare play. "The bus is now in front of the museum. Everyone walk out quietly, in single file please." Then, raising his voice to a triumphant shout continued, "But don't board the bus until Miss Dennis and myself have done a head count."

The children shuffled out through the large, carved wooden doors, down the steps and waited by the bus as they had been told. Wilf had walked out behind Molly Pogson which was a dream come true - for some reason that he couldn't quite understand he'd thought about Molly all the time during the last three months, and whenever she stood near him he felt all funny: his heart fluttered and his legs went weak, but he never told anyone how he felt, putting it down to a virus he might have caught. What Wilf didn't know was that, like all secrets, it was about to be found out as Burp had noticed his friend's big soppy grin when stood behind Molly.

"What's the stupid smile for?" asked Burp, as though he didn't know.

"What stupid smile?" replied Wilf, unaware that he was smiling from ear to ear and his eyes looked like a puppy's.

"This smile," mimicked Burp, fluttering his eyelids and giving a stupid smile.

16

"I'm not doing that."

"Yes you are."

"No I'm not!"

"You are, you fancy Molly Pogson, don't you?"

"No I don't."

"Do!"

"Don't!"

"Do!"

"Quiet, you two!" shouted Miss Dennis as she touched Wilf and Burp on their heads to count them. "Alright children, you can get on the bus now." Everyone climbed noisily aboard. "Quietly!" shouted Miss Dennis.

All of the group found a seat. Wilf and Burp sat in front of Molly and her best friend, Kirsty Armitage, who, unknown to Wilf, Burp fancied like mad. Both lads sat quietly for a while, trying to think of something to say to the girls that might impress them. Burp came up with an idea first. He turned round and pushed his head through the gap between the seats.

"Hey, Molly," he said with a big grin. "Don't put your head near this gap – if Wilf farts he could take your eye out!"

Wilf was so horrified that his eyes opened so wide that if they'd opened any wider his eyeballs would have dropped out onto the floor. He punched Burp's arm.

"Ouch! What was that for?"

"What did you say that to Molly for?"

"It was a joke."

"Listen, Burp, I don't want anyone to know I've swallowed that stone thingy. What if it's worth thousands of pounds? If the police find out they might accuse me of stealing it and lock me up."

"It's a little piece of stone, Wilf. It's not worth anything."

"And how would you know? Listen, you must promise me that you won't tell anyone. It's our secret, ok?" Burp was still rubbing his arm, trying to get the blood circulating again.

"Ok then," he said. Wilf knew that if Burp said he'd keep a secret then he would.

"Why thank you, young man. Oh, I'm sorry about your arm."

"It's ok, I'm sorry about your arm, too." Wilf looked puzzled.

"But my arm's ok."

"It's not now," said Burp and quickly punched Wilf. "Quits!" Both lads sat quietly for a minute. "Well, do you fancy Molly then?" asked Burp.

"Shh!" said Wilf. "She might hear you."

"If you tell me, I'll tell you who I fancy," offered Burp, keen to know.

"Honest?" replied Wilf, unaware that Burp fancied anyone.

"Honest," said Burp, putting his hand on his heart.

"Well, I'm not sure if I fancy her, it's just that I can't stop thinking about her, and when she stands near me my body goes all funny."

"I know what you mean," said Burp.

"You mean she makes you feel like that too?" asked Wilf, wondering whether Molly was carrying a strange virus that made people feel weak whenever she stood next to them.

"Not Molly, turd brain."

"Who then?"

"Promise not to laugh if I tell you?"

"I promise, I promise," said Wilf, eager to find out just who this mystery girl was.

"It's not Molly, it's..." whispered Burp, then stopped for a moment.

"Go on," said Wilf, getting excited at the thought of who it could be.

"You do promise you won't laugh?" Wilf put his hand on his heart.

"May I pee through my nose if I laugh," he promised. Burp leaned over to Wilf's ear.

"It's not Molly, it's her best friend..." he whispered.

"KIRSTY?!" screamed Wilf in shock. Burp looked just as horrified as Wilf had done when he'd made the stupid joke about the fart. Even worse, Kirsty put her head through the gap in the seats.

"Yes?" she asked.

"Nothing," said Wilf with an innocent look. Kirsty looked puzzled.

"But you've just shouted my name." Wilf shook his head.

"No, I didn't."

"Yes, you did."

"No, I was just asking Burp if he was thirsty." Kirsty shook her head, muttered something under her breath, then sat back in her seat. "Phew, that was close," whispered Wilf to Burp who was still in a state of shock. When he came to his senses he punched Wilf's arm again. "Ouch! Stop doing that will you?" growled Wilf.

"What did you scream her name out like that for, you nugget nut?"

"I'm sorry Burp, I was so surprised that it just blurted out before I knew what I was doing." Both lads sat quietly again.

"What are we going to do, then?" asked Burp.

"About what?"

"About Molly and Kirsty, you dimbo."

"I don't know, young man, have you any ideas?"

"We could let them know we like them."

"What?!" screamed Wilf. It was Molly who pushed her head through the gap in the seats this time.

"I didn't say anything," she said, thinking that Wilf had been talking to her.

"Er... I was just telling Burp that I was hot. Don't you think it's hot?" Molly shook her head and sat back in her seat.

"Oh, well done Wilf. Molly and Kirsty are going to think we're a right couple of nutters now." Burp slumped back into his seat while Wilf stared out of the window.

"I wish Molly and Kirsty would just chat to us," he thought out loud. As he said this he got a strange feeling deep in his stomach, as though he'd swallowed a bee which was still buzzing around. He clutched his belly.

"What's wrong?" asked Burp.

"I've got a strange feeling in my belly."

"Is it Molly again?"

"Not that kind of feeling, donkey head. It must be that stone thingy moving around."

"Are you alright?"

"Yeah, it's stopped now." Just as Wilf said this Molly poked her head through the gap between the seats again.

"Would you two like a sweet?" she asked.

Wilf and Burp looked at each other and smiled.

"Yes, please!" they both said together. Wilf held out his hand and Molly gently placed a sweet on his palm.

"I can't believe that this is happening!" he thought to himself as his legs went all wobbly. Wilf looked over at Burp who had sweat on his top lip as Kirsty handed him a sweet.

"What did you think of the museum?" asked Molly. For some reason Wilf's mouth had dried up.

"Wubbish," he said as his tongue stuck to the roof of his mouth. Molly hadn't noticed that Wilf couldn't speak properly.

"Oh, I don't know. I thought it was quite interesting," she said, smiling. He couldn't believe his luck. Not only was Molly Pogson talking to him, she was also smiling as well!

"I mean, some of it was rubbish, but some of it was quite interesting as well," said Wilf, hoping to keep the conversation going.

"Which part did you like the most then, Wilf?" asked Molly.

"He really liked that stone bean thingy, didn't you Wilf?" said Burp, butting into the conversation.

Wilf just smiled then gave Burp a kick when the girls weren't looking.

"I don't remember that," said Kirsty. "But I've bought a book from the museum which has all the exhibits in. We can all have a look together later on if you like."

The two lads nodded, just like the toy dogs you see

on the back shelves of cars, and it wasn't long before the four of them were chatting away like old friends.

"Right, you lot," said Miss Dennis. "We're coming up to school now."

Wilf couldn't believe they were back at school already; it didn't seem like two minutes since they had left Manchester.

"Make sure that you've all got your coats and bags when you get off the bus," said Miss Dennis.

Kirsty tapped Burp on the shoulder.

"Have we all to look at my book after lunch, then?"

"Yes," he replied, without having to give it a second thought.

"Will you be there too, Wilf?" asked Molly.

"Of course I will," he said, sounding a little more keen than he would have liked.

They stood up to get off the bus.

"Sexton! Dawson! To my office! I haven't forgotten, you know." It was old Mr Thomas. He might not have forgotten, but the lads had.

"Oh, dear!" said Burp. "You'll have to think of one of your best excuses, Wilf."

"I'm working on it right now, young man."

"Just make sure it's a good one."

"Have I ever let you down yet, young man?" With that the two lads got off the bus.

"See you two later!" shouted Molly and Kirsty.

"Yeah, see you back in class," replied Wilf and Burp together before setting off for old Thomas's office, each desperately trying to think of an excuse for having been somewhere they shouldn't.

The two lads sat nervously outside Mr Thomas's office. On the door was a sign which said "THE HEAD". It used to say "THE HEAD TEACHER" but Knuckles Parker, the school bully, had stolen the "TEACHER" sign to prove that he could do whatever he liked - and Knuckles *always* did as he liked.

He was built like a Chieftain tank, and had the same effect on people. He once shaved all his hair off so he would look more like his hero, Mike Tyson, but he doesn't like Tyson anymore. Knuckles says that only a sissy would bite off a bit of someone's ear; a real man would have bitten the whole ear off! Yes, Knuckles wasn't happy unless he could hear someone screaming in pain.

Actually, the sign saying "THE HEAD" was just right for old Thomas as that's how people saw him - just one big head with a huge, red nose and a stupid hair style.

"Don't you think that the way old Thomas combs his hair over his bald patch and then sprays it with something that looks and smells like furniture polish makes it look like a piecrust?" asked Wilf. Burp laughed.

"Yeah," he said. "If you stamped on his toe, I wonder

23

if his hair would go up and down like a pedal bin lid?" Both lads burst out laughing.

"That would be ace!" said Wilf. "Can you imagine his hair flapping up and down as he spoke? It would look like he was talking out of the top of his head. I wish that would happen, it would be so funny." Just as Wilf spoke he got that strange buzzing feeling in his stomach again, only this time it felt more painful. He clutched his belly.

"What's wrong?" asked Burp.

"Nothing," said Wilf, not wanting his friend to think he was still worried about the stone thingy.

The door to Thomas's office opened and Miss Williams, the school secretary, came out. She was a horrible woman who seemed to hate children. Tall and thin, she wore thick, horned-rimmed glasses. Her hair was so tightly permed that it looked like she had a bird's nest on top of her head. Her mouth, covered in bright red lipstick which went over the line of her lips, looked as if someone had squashed a tomato there. None of her clothes seemed to fit; her skirts were always too tight and short and her polo-neck jumpers, which she wore to hide her long, scrawny neck, looked too big.

Burp claimed that she looked as though someone had shoved a pump up her bum and sucked all the air out of her body! Wilf agreed - she did look a little like a half-deflated balloon.

Everyone knew that Miss Williams fancied Mr Thomas; everyone except Mr Thomas. All he knew was that he loved himself.

"Mr Thomas will see you two little horrors now," said Miss Williams, hardly moving her lips.

24

"I think she works off batteries," said Wilf as they watched Miss Williams waddle down the corridor to her office.

Burp nervously knocked on the door and heard a loud, theatrical voice from the other side.

"Enter!"

Each tried to push the other in first. After a quick shove in the back from Burp, Wilf went flying into the room, almost falling on the floor. Burp shuffled in behind with a huge grin on his face.

"Ah, it's the troublesome twosome. Come forth, young men."

Once inside, Wilf and Burp couldn't believe what they were seeing: as old Thomas spoke his hair was flapping up and down like a pedal bin lid, just as they had talked about earlier!

"Come hither and stand before me, you wretched creatures!" boomed old Thomas, his hair still flapping up and down to every word he spoke. "Now pray do tell what your pathetic little excuse is for not being with your class." Both lads were dumb-struck; neither could take their eyes off old Thomas's amazing flapping hair style. "Well, I'm waiting!" shouted Mr Thomas, growing a little impatient.

The shock wearing off, Wilf and Burp knew it was going to be a bad time for them as they could now see the funny side of it, or should we say the funny top of it.

"W... well, I... it's... ha... ha..." spluttered Wilf, putting his hand over his mouth to stop himself from laughing any more.

"Do you find something funny, boy?" bellowed Mr Thomas, jumping to his feet. But the more he shouted, the higher his hair rose.

25

Wilf now had both hands over his mouth, tears of laughter rolling down his cheeks. He couldn't speak; the best he could manage was to shake his head from side to side and make a high-pitched squeak. Mr Thomas turned to Burp.

"And what about you, Dawson? Do you find this funny too?" Burp had, up until now, stopped himself from laughing by biting his lips together, but the tears rolling down his face and his shoulders heaving up and down were a dead give-away. He was laughing like crazy on the inside, but trying not to show it on the outside.

"Well, Dawson? Answer me, boy. Do you find this funny as well?" Mr Thomas was now shouting so loud that his hair was flipping from one side of his head to the other then back again, like a speedo needle in a racing car.

Wilf let out a big snotty snort - that was it, the lads could take no more and both collapsed in a heap on the floor. They were no longer scared of old Thomas. How could they possibly be scared of someone whose hair flapped up and down like a one-winged bird trying to take off?

"I command you to stop!!" screamed Mr Thomas. But the more angry he became, the more stupid he looked. His voice had now lost its usual deep, theatrical boom and had turned into a high-pitched, girly scream. "Get out of my office you ignorant little hooligans, and come back at four o'clock. I shall 'phone your parents - we'll see if they can make you show a little respect."

The lads got up off the floor and left with tears streaming down their cheeks, clutching their stomachs. As they came out Miss Williams, waiting to go in, mistook their tears of laughter as tears of pain. This made her feel happy and

27

her chest swelled with pride for Mr Thomas.

"What a man! He knew how to punish children properly," she thought to herself as she walked into his office and closed the door. Seconds later, Wilf and Burp heard a high-pitched scream from inside.

"I think she's just seen old Thomas's piecrust, young man," said Wilf, crying with laughter. Burp was doubled-up on the floor, holding his stomach. He was laughing but no sound came out.

"Stop, please stop now!" begged Burp. "I've got stomach ache with laughing so much."

"Me, too!" gasped Wilf. "Let's go outside and get some fresh air." They staggered down the corridor, still snorting and sniggering, and went out through the main entrance to sit on the steps leading down to the drive. When they'd calmed down a bit Wilf turned to Burp.

"How on earth did that happen?"

"I don't know, but it wasn't half funny," said Burp, wiping the tears from his face. The lads looked at each other then burst out laughing again.

However, their laughter was to be short-lived as Knuckles Parker and his side kick, Snotty Kennedy, had spotted them.

28

"Oi! Yous two! Come 'ere!" Wilf and Burp looked up to see the two large, imposing figures of Knuckles and Snotty.

"Oh, no!" groaned Burp. "That's all we need just now."

Knuckles was busy hammering his right fist into the palm of his left hand. Snotty, who got his name because he always seemed to have a snotty bogey hanging from his nose, was actually bigger than Knuckles but far more stupid, if that was possible. Snotty had always hero-worshipped Knuckles, who in turn treated him like his own pet bear.

"Gi' us yer money!" growled Knuckles. Quite why he spoke like this no one knew. His dad was a doctor and his mum a teacher and when they, or any teachers, were about he always spoke in a posh voice. But if left alone with any other kids for some reason Knuckles turned into a cave-man. He thought that this growling voice made him sound menacing; actually he was right, it did!

"We haven't got any money," said Wilf.

"You won't 'ave any teef if yer don't gi'us some money!" growled Snotty, who then had to let his brain rest for a while after such a long sentence.

29

"I'm telling you we haven't any money, honest. Look!" said Wilf, turning his pockets inside out.

"Wot about you," said Snotty to Burp, his brain working again after the short rest.

"Look - empty!" said Burp, who had also turned his pockets inside out. Actually, Wilf and Burp did have some money, but they had learned through experience that the best place to keep it was in their socks. That way *they* got to spend it, not Knuckles and Snotty.

"Right then, if yer 'ave no money, yer'll 'ave to do a forfeit," snapped Knuckles.

"What kind of forfeit would that be?" asked Burp.

"Yer 'ave to go round the back of old Thomas's office, then pull yer trousers down an' show yer bums through his window."

"No way!" cried Burp.

"Wot yer say?" asked Knuckles.

"I said there's no way that you'll make me do that, turnip brain!" This confused Knuckles, because no one had ever said "no" to him before. Wilf was even more confused; he had got used to his head being that shape and size, and thought it would be a shame if Knuckles changed it for him.

Wilf hissed at Burp through gritted teeth.

"Burp, shut up! We're both going to get killed here." Burp, however, gave Wilf an evil grin then took up a karate stance.

Now Wilf had known for some time that Burp had been going to karate lessons but had never actually seen him do any, and Burp was not the kind of person to brag about it. But that said, Wilf didn't think this was the best time to show that he was Bruce Lee.

What happened next, though, surprised Wilf. Burp started to wave his arms as though he was trying to catch a fly, then made a strange noise that sounded like a chicken laying an extra-large egg. Finally, with a loud scream, Burp spun round and ran off. Wilf was so surprised, as were Knuckles and Snotty, that he just stood there. Then Snotty caught hold of Wilf and with his big, bear-like arms squeezed him tightly round his chest.

"Wot yer gonna do now, Sexton?" growled Snotty. Wilf gasped as the air was squeezed out of his lungs.

"Ok, Snotty, will you stop when you hear my ribs crack, please?"

"Don't call me Snotty!" grunted Snotty.

"But I don't know your real name," gasped Wilf.

"It's Malcolm." Wilf thought that at any other time he might find this name funny, but not just now.

"Well, Malcolm, and… er, Mr Knuckles, I wish you'd show me some compassion and let me keep my face the way it is," said Wilf, his lips turning blue through lack of oxygen.

Then it happened again. Wilf felt that strange buzzing feeling in his stomach, but this time it was quite painful.

"I'm so sorry Wilf, are you ok?" asked Snotty, letting him go. "I didn't mean to hurt yer."

"Yes, we never stopped to think what effect our actions would have on you," added Knuckles, using his posh voice. "Come over here, Wilf, and sit down and try to get your breath back." Knuckles helped Wilf over to the steps that led in to school. Wilf thought that it must be some sort of trick, but having a much-needed sit down seemed like a good

31

idea. "How can we ever make up for what we have done?" asked Knuckles, still using the voice that he kept for his parents and teachers.

Wilf thought he'd try his luck.

"Er... you couldn't lend me fifty pence, could you?" he requested, closing his eyes and putting his hands over his head, waiting for Knuckles or Snotty to give him a whack.

"Er... I don't have fifty pence in change, I'm afraid. Would a pound be ok?" Wilf couldn't believe what he'd just heard. He looked at Knuckles, who really seemed to be concerned.

"Er... yeah, that'll be fine," he replied, not quite sure what was happening. It seemed as though the school bullies were actually showing him some compassion.

As Knuckles was handing the pound to Wilf he heard a noise from behind.

"Eeeeagh!" Suddenly, Burp came flying over Wilf's head and karate-kicked Knuckles in the chest. Knuckles staggered backwards and Burp started making the noise like a chicken laying the unusually-large egg again, putting his fists up to fight.

"No one picks on my friend and gets away with it!" cried Burp, trying to sound Chinese.

"Oh, no!" thought Wilf. "Burp, stop! You don't understand. We're friends now - I hope!" shouted Wilf, trying to prevent his friend from being killed.

"Stand back, Wilf, we don't want to hurt you," growled Knuckles!"

"Yeah, but we're gonna hurt *him*!" grunted Snotty.

Lots of thoughts started to race through Wilf's head:

why had Knuckles and Snotty showed him compassion, and how had old Thomas's hair flapped up and down? And what about Molly and Kirsty making friends just like that? Then there was that strange feeling he got in his stomach. What had caused all these things?

"It's because I wished for them to happen!" he suddenly realised.

Meanwhile, Snotty had hold of Burp round his neck.

"Hold him still while I punch him!" shouted Knuckles.

Wilf decided that the only way to test his theory was to make a wish.

"I wish that Knuckles and Snotty were really scared of Burp," he shouted. Almost immediately, Wilf felt the same strange buzzing in his stomach as before, but this time it was so painful that he fell to the ground clutching his belly.

Burp couldn't see Wilf, owing to his head being stuck under Snotty's armpit, but he'd heard his friend shout out the wish.

"Can't you think of something a bit more helpful than that?" said Burp in a muffled voice as Snotty tried to bend his neck into a position that it wasn't meant to go into.

Wilf had now got back to his feet. He still had the pain in his stomach, but not as bad.

It was then that a look of horror came over Knuckles's face. He pointed to Burp, who was still stuck under Snotty's sweaty armpit.

"Snotty! Have you seen who you're trying to strangle?" he screamed as he turned and ran off. Snotty slowly looked under his arm and came eye to eye with Burp.

"Hello, Malcolm!" gasped Burp. "Do you know that

33

your armpit smells like meat and onion pie?" Snotty let go of Burp straight away and his face turned white with fear as though he'd just seen a ghost.

"I'm v... very sorry, Burp, I'd never 'ave grabbed hold of you if I'd known who yer were," stuttered Snotty, his legs now shaking with real fear. He dropped to his knees and grabbed hold of Burp's leg. "Please don't hurt me!" he cried. Burp was confused and angry as he thought Knuckles and Snotty were having a laugh at his expense.

"Just get lost, Snotty!" he said, his pride dented. Snotty jumped to his feet and ran away as fast as he could.

"Did you see that, Burp? Did you?" shouted Wilf, getting very excited. "Whatever I wish for comes true. Did you hear me? I said whatever I wish for comes true!"

"Oh yeah, sure, and I've got a dragon that eats fish and custard sandwiches," replied Burp, thinking Wilf must have had a blow to the head to say something so ridiculous.

"Ok, then, what about old Thomas's hair flapping around? I wished for that - and Molly and Kirsty talking to us, I wished for that as well."

"They were just coincidences."

"Then why did those two idiots show me compassion when I wished for it, then? Look, Knuckles actually gave me a pound!"

"You're talking rubbish now, young man. Have you had a bump on the head?" asked Burp, wishing that Wilf would change the subject. Wilf, however, wasn't very happy. Not only did he still have the pain in his stomach, but also his best friend didn't believe what he was saying.

"Ok, then, explain how all these things happened?"

Well, think about it," said Burp. "Molly and Kirsty have probably alway fancied us, and who could blame them? Today was likely the day they chose to pluck up the courage to talk to us."

"And what about old Thomas's amazing flapping hair-do?

"I don't know. Maybe there was a draught in his office."

"A draught! His hair moved up and down to the sound of his voice," said Wilf, thinking that Burp was talking rubbish. "And what about the creatures from the black lagoon showing me some compassion, then?"

"Maybe they're just sick of beating people up."

"Well it didn't stop them from beating you up, did it?" And when I wished for them to be scared of you, what happened? They ran away, didn't they." Burp thought for a moment.

"Maybe they'd heard about me having karate lessons," he said, not really convincing himself. Burp knew that Knuckles and Snotty would ask Mike Tyson for his dinner money, so him having karate lessons wouldn't bother them at all. "Ok then, great mystical one, prove it!"

"Prove what?"

"Prove that when you make a wish it comes true."

"How?"

"By making a wish, putty brain."

Wilf wasn't that keen to make another wish. He already had a bad pain in his stomach, and he knew that every time he made a wish the pain got worse.

"Not just now," he said. Burp laughed.

"See, I said you were talking rubbish." This really got

35

up Wilf's nose - he had to prove it once and for all.

"Ok, then. What would you like me to wish for?" asked Wilf. Burp thought for a moment.

"It's got to be something that we can't put down to coincidence."

"Like what?" asked Wilf.

"I don't know. Make me fly or something."

"Ok, then. I wish that Burp could fly." As Wilf spoke the pain got worse this time; it wasn't a buzzing but more like a burning feeling, and his stomach was so heavy that he couldn't stand up. He felt so bad that tears welled up in his eyes. "Burp, help me!" he cried, curling up on the floor. Burp, however, couldn't hear since he was floating in the air ten feet above.

"Good grief, young man, I think you're right. You *can* make wishes come true! Now could you get me down before I float away to Mars," he said, looking down at his friend on the floor. Wilf could hardly talk owing to the pain. "Wilf, get me down, I'm floating away!" screamed Burp, suddenly panicking. Wilf, unable to think straight because he was hurting so much, just wanted Burp to help him.

"I wish you would help me, Burp, instead of messing around," he said in a faint whisper. With that a screaming pain shot through his body and Wilf passed out. Burp floated back down.

"Wilf, are you ok?" He shook his friend's limp body. "Wilf, talk to me. Don't mess about." Worried, Burp could see that Wilf had turned deathly white and his lips were going blue. "You'll be ok, Wilf, I'll get help!" he shouted and ran up the steps into school.

36

Burp ran along the corridor to Mr Thomas's office and charged in without knocking. Inside, Miss Williams was trying to fasten one of her hair grips to the side of Mr Thomas's head in an attempt to stop his hair from flapping up and down.

"Sir, Sir, come quick! It's Wilf, he's very ill!" shouted Burp, almost in tears.

"Not you again, boy!" screamed old Thomas as the hair grip gave way and his hair flew up like a circus clown's wig. "Get out!"

"Yes, get out!" shouted skinny Williams as well.

"But Sir, you don't understand," continued Burp, tears now filling his eyes. He was sure that if he didn't get help soon his friend would die. "It's Wilf, Sir, he's collapsed outside!"

"Another of your childish pranks, Dawson. Well, we'll see how funny you think you are when your father calls this afternoon. Now get out of my sight!"

Burp burst into tears.

"Please, you must listen to me, I'm not joking!" Miss Williams grabbed hold of Burp by his ear and marched him out of the office.

37

"Go on, you horrible child," she sneered, pushing Burp down the corridor. He ran off as fast as he could and half-way down bumped into Molly and Kirsty. They were just about to say "hi" when Burp grabbed them.

"It's Wilf, come quick, he's very ill!" The three of them ran outside. Wilf was curled up on the floor, motionless. A small crowed had gathered round him and kneeling beside the limp body was Knuckles Parker. He was crying and gently holding Wilf's head.

"Someone please help. Show some compassion." Then he saw Burp. "Please, Burp, don't hurt me, I'm trying to help my friend."

Everyone looked on in disbelief, for Knuckles was usually the sort of person who stole from someone when they had collapsed. In fact, Knuckles was usually to blame for people collapsing.

"What's up with Knuckles?" asked Molly.

"Never mind Knuckles, we need to get help for Wilf," said Burp.

Miss Dennis had seen all the children gathering round, and could see Knuckles on the floor.

"There must be a fight," she thought and ran over to see what was happening. "What's going on here?" she demanded.

"It's Wilf, Miss, he's ill, and Mr Thomas and Miss Williams won't help!" blurted out Burp without taking a breath. Miss Dennis took one look at Wilf and ran into school to 'phone for an ambulance.

Burp sat with Wilf; he was crying and didn't care who saw him.

"You'll be alright, young man, just hold on," he sobbed.

It seemed like an age before the ambulance arrived. The paramedics told everyone to stand back. Burp watched tearfully as they quickly fitted Wilf with an oxygen mask before giving him an injection. Still motionless, Wilf looked pale and cold as they put him into the ambulance. The doors were closed and on went the blue flashing lights, followed by the siren. Burp watched as the ambulance sped off down the school drive and out of sight.

Kirsty walked over to Burp and put her arms round him. If she had cuddled him on any other day it would have been the best day of his life; but not today.

Part Two

The Warrior and The Banshee Queen

Burp was trying to think how all this had started and what could have given Wilf such strange powers. Then his legs went all wobbly because Kirsty had just kissed his cheek.

"Are you alright?" asked Kirsty. Burp still had a few tears trickling down his face, but now he had a great big soppy smile as well.

"Er...ha...mm..." was all that came out. "Good grief!" he thought. "My mouth won't work." Then he moved away from Kirsty, thinking that if she kissed him again he would turn into a big, babbling jelly.

"Did Wilf feel ill this morning?" she asked.

"Well, his stomach did feel a bit dodgy after we'd come out of the museum."

"Maybe it's something he ate?" Then it came to Burp in a flash.

"Of course!" he shouted. "That's it!"

"That's what?" asked Kirsty, a little puzzled.

"Kirsty, have you got the book about the exhibits in the museum?" Burp thought back and realised that all the strange things that had gone on had happened after Wilf

43

swallowed the stone thingy, so it must be the stone thingy now killing him.

"Yes, it's in my locker, but I don't expect you to look at it now, not with everything that's happened this morning."

"Can you go and get it please, as quick as possible." Kirsty thought it strange that Burp wanted to look at the book now, but if it cheered him up then why not. She ran off to get it.

"Why do you want the book, Burp?" asked Molly.

"I can't tell you yet, but I think the answer to Wilf's illness might be in there."

"But it's a book about old Celtic exhibits," she said, now very puzzled.

Kirsty was on her way back with the book when Knuckles and Snotty stopped her.

"Wot yer got there?" asked Snotty, hoping that he'd got all the words in the right order.

"It's a book, full of words, so it's of no use to you!" said Kirsty, snubbing them both.

"Oh, ok then. 'Bye," said Snotty, not realising that he had just been snubbed.

"Wait a minute, gi' us dat book!" demanded Knuckles in his moron voice.

"No! Burp wants to see it," replied Kirsty, not at all scared of the two idiots.

"Not Burp Dawson?" Knuckles and Snotty shouted out together.

"Yes, Burp Dawson!" replied Kirsty, getting angry with the idiots.

"We're very sorry. Please don't tell Burp that we

stopped you!" begged Knuckles.

"Just get out of my way, will you?" she snapped. Knuckles and Snotty ran off, leaving her feeling very puzzled. She went to find Burp and Molly. "Here's the book," Kirsty said, holding it up. She handed it to Burp.

"Thanks," he said, quickly thumbing through.

"On the way back I was stopped by those idiots Parker and Kennedy," said Kirsty.

"What did they want?" asked Molly.

"The book, until I mentioned your name, Burp. Then they got frightened and ran off. Why?" Burp stopped looking through the book and smiled. This was a good chance to impress Kirsty.

"It's because I do karate."

"You must be very good to scare those two," she said.

"Well, let's just say that some people know me as Bruce Dawson," bragged Burp.

"Bruce who?" asked Kirsty, not knowing about Bruce Lee.

"Never mind," sighed Burp, realising that he'd failed to impress. He began thumbing through the book again. "Here it is!" he said, stopping at page nine.

There, in the bottom right hand corner of the page, was a picture of the stone bean thingy. Underneath was a caption which read: "The stone of Orf, believed by the ancient Celts to have magical powers. Also believed by some to be able to open the mythical tomb of Tara where the cauldron of life was said to be hidden."

"That's it! That's what's causing Wilf's illness," he shouted. Both girls looked at the picture, then at Burp, then

45

back at each other.

"What are you talking about?" asked Molly.

"Wilf swallowed that stone by accident." The girls burst out laughing.

"Just how did he manage that?" asked Molly.

"He had it in his mouth when old Thomas made him jump," replied Burp. The girls burst out laughing again.

"If you don't mind me asking, just what was he doing with it in his mouth in the first place?" laughed Kirsty. Burp realised just how idiotic he would look if he told them the full story, so he just smiled.

"It's a long story, but the magic in the stone is killing Wilf. I must get to the hospital and tell them," he said. Molly shook her head in disbelief. Taking the book off Burp she pointed to it.

"Look, do you see that word there? It says "mythology". M.Y.T.H.O.L.O.G.Y. That means it's not true - understand? It's a myth!"

"And I'm telling you it *is* true. The stone really is magical. I've seen it work, and I'm off to the hospital to tell them." Burp ran off down the school drive.

"Burp, come back! You'll get into awful trouble for running out of school," shouted Kirsty after him, but it was too late; Burp was gone. Molly shrugged her shoulders.

"I'm not surprised that nature chose women to have children. Can you imagine giving a child to something as stupid as a man?" she said turning to Kirsty, who nodded in agreement.

46

7

From his office, old Thomas saw Burp running out of school. He opened his window.

"Dawson, just where do you think you're going, young man?" he shouted.

"I'm off to save my friend, which is more than you would do!" Burp shouted back.

"Come here this instant!" shouted Thomas, his hair still flapping up and down like a one-winged bird.

"Oh, shut up, and keep your hair on, slap head!" replied Burp. He no longer cared about anything except getting to the hospital to save his friend.

Once out of the school grounds he ran down Fernlee Mount Road to the bus stop by the corner shop. He checked his socks to see how much money he had and counted up: one pound fifty.

"That should be enough to get to the hospital," he thought. He knew that the 373 stopped here and also outside the hospital.

After waiting what seemed like an eternity the bus finally arrived. Burp held out his arm as far as it would stretch so the bus would stop, but the driver just sneered at the lad, put his foot down and sped off. Burp went crazy.

"You idiot, you moron, I hope that you suffer from diarrhoea for the rest of your life!" he screamed after the bus. But it carried on along Fernlee Mount Road and disappeared from sight down Fleming Hill. "Oh, no! What am I going to do now?" he wondered.

It was then that a stroke of luck, and genius, occurred. The stroke of luck was when an ambulance passed by Fernlee Mount Road and the stroke of genius when Burp pretended to faint.

The ambulance stopped and the paramedics got out. They asked Burp what had happened but he didn't answer; he just lay there, his body limp. It has to be said that it did look as though he really was ill, despite overdoing the moaning.

"We'd better take him to hospital and get him checked over," said one of the paramedics. Burp was so happy to hear those words he could have kissed him, but thought it better not to. They quickly put the boy on a stretcher and into the ambulance which set off with its lights flashing and siren blazing.

"Ah... this is the only way to travel!" thought Burp as he laid on his back looking out of the window, watching the roof tops flash by.

The ambulance soon reached the hospital where, without warning, the doors swung open and lots of people rushed in shouting things like, "Take him to resus., what's his b.p.?" Burp thought he'd be better off moaning and keeping his eyes closed. He was taken to a small room where there were lots of serious looking machines and thought that it was probably a good time to come round so he opened his eyes.

"Where am I?" he moaned.

"It's ok, you're going to be fine," said a woman with something resembling a miner's lamp attached to her head. Burp would have burst out laughing had he not noticed the seriously large needle in her hand. He sat up, thinking now would be a good time to get out of the place.

"Is there anyone we can contact for you?" asked the woman with the miner's lamp.

"Yes," replied Burp in a feeble voice.

"Who?" The nurse put her ear close to Burp's mouth.

"Scottie," he whispered.

"Did you say Scottie?" she asked, thinking that Burp was about to faint again.

"Yes," he gasped, as though about to breathe his last, then shouted, "Because I want him to beam me up!" With this he jumped off the bed and made a run for it.

After giving the nurse the slip he ran through the hospital until he came to the main reception area. Walking over to the information desk Burp saw a sign which said "ring for attention" and pressed the buzzer.

A man sat behind the desk sorting out mail stopped for a moment, glanced up at Burp, then carried on working. Burp checked himself, just to make sure he hadn't turned invisible (which he hadn't), then gave a little cough to let the man know he was waiting. Again the man glanced up, and again ignored Burp. This really maddened the young lad; why do adults always treat kids as if they don't exist?

Then he put his finger on the buzzer and left it there.

"Oi, stop that now!" shouted the man. Burp glanced

his way but ignored him.

"Now he knows what it feels like," he thought.

"I said stop that!" shouted the man again.

"Who, me?" asked Burp, still with his finger on the buzzer. "There's nothing quite like a buzzer for making you visible," he thought. The man pushed Burp's finger away.

"What do you want?" he growled.

"Er... I'm looking for someone who came in this morning. His name's Wilf Sexton."

"Is he a relative?" Burp thought for a moment. If he said "no" the grumpy old bloke wouldn't give him any information.

"Yes, he's my brother." Then Burp got a bit carried away. "Actually, he's my twin brother, and when he's in pain I feel it as well." Burp clutched his stomach and screwed his face up as though he was in real agony. "My brother must be so ill," said Burp, still acting like someone had punched him.

The man stared, unsure as to whether the boy was telling the truth. He decided to give Burp the benefit of the doubt; after all, if he was telling the truth and was to faint there in front of his desk, just think of all the paperwork that it might involve.

"He's in ward five," revealed the man, staring at his computer. "That's to your left, then down to the end of the corridor."

"Thank you," groaned Burp and shuffled off, still clutching his stomach and moaning, "Oh! Ah!" with every step.

"Phew!" thought the man. "Let him pass out somewhere else. It's not as if I don't have enough paperwork to do."

Arriving at ward five, Burp thought it better to stick to his story about being related to Wilf. He pressed the buzzer on the door, which was opened after a minute or two, and there in front of him stood a huge woman - a sumo wrestler in a nurse's uniform. She looked down at Burp, her face grim, then suddenly broke into a huge smile, the kind which makes others who see it want to smile.

"Yes, my love, how can I help you?" she asked in a lovely, soft, Irish accent.

"Er... I've come to see my brother," lied Burp, unable to take his eyes off the woman's huge, smiling face.

"Your brother?" asked the nurse, looking a little puzzled.

"Yes. Well, actually he's my twin brother." Now this was a big mistake on Burp's part, because there was a serious flaw in what he was saying and he was about to find out what.

"And what do they call your brother, then?" the sumo nurse asked him.

"Wilf... Wilf Sexton."

"And your name is?"

"Burp Sexton," he lied again. "She can't catch me out that easily," he thought.

"So it's little Wilf Sexton, your twin brother, that you've come to see, is it?" said the nurse, trying to keep a straight face. "You'd better follow me, then." She waddled off down the ward, Burp behind. Just before they got to the bed where Wilf was the nurse stopped.

"Now, don't be frightened by all the machines round your twin, they're there to help him, but I don't think that he'll be able to talk to you, my love," she said, leading Burp to

51

Wilf's bed. "Here he is, my love." She pointed to a room with just one bed by itself.

Burp walked in and couldn't believe what he saw; Wilf lay there with pipes up his nose and in his arms, his face white as snow, his eyes shut, not moving a muscle.

"Is he… going to die?" stuttered Burp as tears welled up in his eyes. The nurse put her big, soft arms round Burp.

"Don't you worry, my love," she said softly. "The doctors will find out what's wrong with him."

"*I* know what's wrong with him," said Burp.

"What's that then, my love?"

"He's swallowed a magic bean." Burp could hear how stupid he sounded as the words came out of his mouth.

"Well, if it's in there I'm sure the doctors will find it," she said, trying to calm Burp.

"I like this woman," he thought to himself. "He looks so pale," said Burp to the nurse.

"Yes, you certainly have a lot more colour than your twin," she replied.

It was then that Burp realised just how stupid he'd been. You see Burp and Wilf had been friends all their lives. They dressed the same: white t-shirts with blue stripes, big baggy shorts which they wore below the knee, and spot trainers; their families were best friends - Burp's father worked with Wilf's, both joiners on building sites; the two families even went away on holidays together, so in a way Wilf and Burp were brothers - except Wilf's family were Irish, while Burp's were West Indian. Wilf was pale even when he was well, and Burp was black.

The boy shook his head.

52

"Yeah, the colour has drained out of him, you'd think he was a white boy."

"That must be it," said the nurse, looking at Burp with a smile. He smiled back, knowing she didn't believe him. "You can have five minutes with him. Ok, my love?" Burp nodded and the nurse left the room.

He leaned over his friend.

"Wilf, can you hear me? Can you speak? You must wish the stone thingy out of you." Wilf didn't move or speak, he just lay there. Burp could hear the bleep, bleep of the machines connected to his best friend. He gently put his hand on Wilf's shoulder. "Wilf!" he said, tears trickling down his cheeks. "Can you hear me?"

What Burp didn't know was that deep in Wilf's head something very, very strange was happening. He was no longer in hospital but what seemed to be a huge castle, floating in space. The ceiling was so high that he could hardly see it and on both sides were rows of huge stone arches which seemed to go on forever.

Stood in one of the arches to his left was a powerfully-built man with long hair wearing a leather waistcoat and a kilt. He had bands around the tops of his arms which looked to be made from beans like the one Wilf had swallowed. On his back was a bow and a quiver full of arrows, and in one hand he carried a bronze shield, like the one in the museum. In the other he held a sword that looked so sharp Wilf felt as though he could cut himself just by looking at it.

To Wilf's right was his mum; at least he thought it was his mum. It certainly looked like her: she was small and slim with long blonde hair, her face pale, dressed in a long flowing gown. It was this that made Wilf nervous. Why would his mum dress like that? There was something different about her, something strange, but he couldn't work out what it was.

"Quickly, come to me, Wilf!" called his mum in a soft voice.

"No! Don't listen to her, she is not who she appears to be. She is evil - she is the banshee queen!" shouted the man with the sword. "All she wants is the Orf stone which you have. Once she has it she will kill you!"

Wilf didn't know what to do. He didn't want to upset the man with the sword, that would be silly. And there was something strange about his mum, something eerie, although he could do with a cuddle right now since his legs were shaking with fear.

"Come to me," called his mum again in a calm, soothing voice. "Come to me, let me hold you." Wilf felt hypnotised by her voice and started to walk towards her, following the low, soft voice whispering, "Come to me" as she held out her arms.

Wilf held out his hands to touch her; he looked at her face but suddenly felt so scared. How could he be scared of his own mother whom he loved? He also felt that he couldn't move away, even if he wanted to. Then, as he looked at her face again, he saw the whites of her eyes were turning red; not just any red, but a murderous blood-red. Despite this he still felt helpless and couldn't pull away. His fingers moved closer to hers.

"That's it," she said, "take hold of my hand." A chill ran down Wilf's spine.

"NO!!" screamed the man. Wilf felt something whizz past the side of his head, and heard a blood-curdling "AGGHH… OOHH!!" He looked at what he thought was his mum and froze to the spot - instead of his mum standing in front of him there was a huge, black beast at least seven feet tall with thick, black, matted hair all over its body. On its hands and feet were large, sharp claws but its eyes filled Wilf with most fear - there were no eyeballs, just deep, blood-red slits as though the beast was on fire inside.

Then Wilf saw what had whizzed past his head, for sticking out of the beast's shoulder was an arrow. Sneering, it removed the arrow from its great body. Wilf still couldn't move.

"Come to me, child!" said the beast, but now in a rasping, menacing tone. Wilf felt helpless as he went to take hold of its hand. Then there was another "AGGHH... OOHH!!" as a second arrow hit the beast, this time in the chest, and it fell backwards.

Suddenly the hold over Wilf had been broken and he jumped back to safety. Turning, he saw the man in the kilt preparing his bow to shoot another arrow.

"Stay on the path in the middle. Neither she nor I can tread there, so you will be safe," shouted the man. Wilf was shaking with fear.

"W... who are you?" he stuttered.

"Don't be frightened."

"What's there to be frightened of?" shouted Wilf. "I mean, over there is a huge, hairy beast which until a moment ago was my mum, then there's you, with, if you don't mind me saying, a rather large, threatening bow in your hands!"

"Come over here, there is nothing to fear," said the man, putting down his bow.

"Nothing to fear?!" screamed Wilf. "I'm way past fear, I'm at the 'mum I've got lumps in my undies stage'." The

57

man gave Wilf a cold stare.

"Move away from the banshee and closer to me. I will try to explain what is happening to you."

"And how do I know if I can trust you?"

"So you would rather trust the banshee?" Wilf turned and looked at the wailing banshee and the noise seemed to cut deep into him, leaving the boy afraid and confused.

"Er... good point," said Wilf, trying to act as though he wasn't scared.

"You can stay where you are for now if it makes you feel better," said the man, "but you must not look at, or go near, the banshee."

"Let me think... this is a hard one... you don't want me to go over to the big, black, hairy beast that wants to rip my head off and play hide the thimble. Er... ok - it's a deal, I won't go and play with the big doggy!" The man looked at Wilf with the same cold stare, then spoke again.

"My name is Liam and I am a marsh warrior. I am from a different world to you, as is the banshee."

"Yes, I thought I hadn't seen many of those walking around Huddersfield," said Wilf, pointing at the banshee.

"You must listen to me," said Liam as the banshee let out another blood-curdling scream, making Wilf nearly jump out of his skin. The boy turned to the banshee.

"I wish you'd get lost!"

"NO!" screamed Liam as the beast disappeared from view. "The banshee will have followed your life-force back to your world. We must stop it!"

Burp was still sat next to Wilf's bed, trying to stop himself from crying.

"Please, Wilf, just try to speak!" he pleaded.

"GRRR!"

"What did you say, Wilf? Did you speak?"

"GRRR!"

"What are you trying to say, Wilf?"

"AGGHH... OOHH!!" Turning, Burp realised that the noise was not coming from Wilf, and what he saw scared him so much that he couldn't move or make a sound - just a few feet away from him stood the banshee queen!

It moved slowly towards Burp, like a cat stalking a mouse. He could smell the stench of rotting flesh on its breath as it drew closer. Trying to move out of the way he tripped over a chair, landing on his back. Helpless on the floor, the banshee moved in for the kill. Opening its mouth it revealed brown, blood-stained teeth and those murderous red slits of eyes focused on Burp, who said the first thing that came into his head which happened to be, "Nice doggy!"

Burp didn't yet realise what he was dealing with. The banshee took one of its long, sharp claws and gently stroked it down the side of his face; he suddenly knew that just one swipe from this beast would be enough to finish him.

"What a lovely snack," hissed the banshee. "First you, then your friend, and I will be unbeatable!" It let out a laugh just like a wolf howling at the moon. "Goodbye, child!" it said, raising its huge, powerful arm.

"No! Please don't!" pleaded Burp. But it was too late; the banshee's arm came crashing down onto the boy's head.

"AGGHH... OOHH!" screamed the banshee suddenly as it too was sent sprawling across the room. Getting to its feet it let out a piercing scream then ran and hurled itself

through a glass window separating the rooms, sending glass flying across the ward.

Then Burp saw what had just saved his life - at least he hoped it had saved his life and wasn't going to take over where the banshee had left off. Still sprawled on the floor, Burp looked up and saw in front of him the huge figure of Liam, armed with his sword and shield. The sight of him with his sword drawn was enough to frighten an army.

"Wilf, whatever you're wishing for in your dream, stop wishing for it, please!" whispered Burp, knowing that all this must be something to do with the stone.

"Don't be afraid, I am a friend of Wilf's," said Liam, picking Burp up as though he weighed no more than a piece of paper and gently sitting him on the end of Wilf's bed.

"D... don't try to hurt me; I do karate you know!" stuttered Burp.

"What?" asked Liam.

"Hello, friend of Wilf's," said Burp after staring at Liam's sword and deciding not to talk too much about his karate skills.

"Are you hurt?" asked Liam.

"No, but I think I might have to change my undies soon!" Just then two security men came running into the room, closely followed by a doctor and nurse. "He's a friend. It's ok," shouted Burp, hoping that the security men wouldn't be stupid enough to try and tackle Liam.

"Who are you talking about, and what the heck's going on in here?" asked one of the security men.

"Who am I talking about?!" shouted Burp, thinking they must be blind. "The big guy in the skirt with the sword, dimbo, that's who!" But when Burp turned round he found that Liam had disappeared. "Oh, dear!" he thought. "Now I'm in trouble." Then, without warning, he was grabbed from behind and his eyes covered. He couldn't see who had hold of him, but heard a voice that chilled his blood.

"Guess who, child?" said the menacing voice in a low rasp. "Do you know what I'm going to do to you?"

"D... does it involve removing my head from my

body? Because if it does, please don't tell me," stuttered Burp, shaking with fear.

"No, child, I'm going to… give you a big kiss!" replied the sinister voice, and a big, wet kiss was firmly planted on Burp's forehead. Turning, Burp saw Wilf, stood in his hospital gown.

"You're ok!" shouted Burp, throwing his arms round his friend.

"Get off!" said Wilf in disgust. "I was only joking when I kissed you. I don't fancy you!" The lads looked at each other, glad they were both ok, then burst out laughing.

"Just what is going on in here? And you, how have you recovered so quickly?" asked the doctor, pointing at Wilf.

"I don't know?" said Wilf. "It must have been something I ate!" The two burst out laughing again.

The doctor ordered Wilf to get back into bed and, as he clambered in, the back of his gown opened to reveal his bum to all in the room.

"I'll tell him about that later!" thought Burp. The lads were then quizzed by security about what had happened. Outside the room, hospital staff were busy clearing up the glass.

"Your parents will be here soon," said a nurse sticking her head round the door.

"We'll let you have a rest until they arrive, then we want the truth about what happened. No more fairy stories, ok?" the head of hospital security told them. Both lads nodded as the security men left.

"What was that all about? How *did* you get better?" asked Burp when the two were finally alone.

"Not now, Burp. We've got to get out of here as soon as possible. Pass me my clothes from the cabinet." Burp did as his friend asked and Wilf got dressed under the bed sheets. "How can we get out without anyone seeing us?" Burp went to the window and looked out.

"I know, we can climb through the window and drop down onto that flat roof." So they both scrambled through the window, out onto the roof and found a drain-pipe they could shimmy down, landing at the main entrance to casualty. Unfortunately, they were quickly spotted by the nurse Burp had previously run away from.

"There he is, that's the boy who fooled us earlier!" she shouted. Two ambulance men chased Burp and Wilf, but they were far too old and fat to catch up and the lads gave them the slip by running through someone's back garden.

"And just what have you been up to, young man?" Wilf asked Burp.

"Oh, not much. I just hitched a lift, you know."

"In an ambulance?"

"Yeah."

"The old passing out in the street routine?"

"Yeah."

"I'm proud of you, young man," congratulated Wilf.

"Why, thank you, it's always nice for someone to recognise genius when they see it. Now, will you tell me what on earth is going on?"

"We have to get to Scammonden Reservoir to meet up with Liam; he'll explain everything to you," said Wilf, and the two lads set off walking, keeping away from the main roads in case the police were looking for them.

Part Three

The Explanation

The reservoir was only a few miles from the hospital, set in the heart of the Pennine moors which gave it an eerie sort of beauty. They walked for over an hour before reaching it, and were extremely tired. What a day it had been! They had set off at eight o'clock that morning to go on a school outing, and by four o'clock the same afternoon had ended up outlaws, or so they thought, alone on the moors.

The lads sat quietly by the reservoir, staring at the deep, dark water which reflected the barren yet beautiful landscape surounding it. Both were thinking about all that had happened that day.

"Have I been dreaming, or has this been one heck of a day?" laughed Burp.

"Well, if you've been dreaming I must be having the same dream. And yes, it's been one heck of a day!"

"Neither of you are dreaming," said a voice from behind them. Both jumped with fright and, turning quickly, saw Liam, sword in hand.

"I wish you wouldn't do that!" snapped Burp.

"Do what?" asked Liam.

"Just appear from behind people and start talking. I could've had a heart attack."

"Or poohed your pants," added Wilf.

"Yes, or poohed my pants," agreed Burp. Liam walked over to the lads and stuck his sword into the ground.

"We must talk, there is so much for you to learn and so little time." Wilf got to his feet.

"Can't we go somewhere else? It's getting dark and cold, and I'm hungry."

"Me, too!" agreed Burp. "I'm so hungry I could eat an elephant, trunk and all, and still have room for a pudding."

"You must listen!" said Liam, giving the lads a cold stare. "I did not expect the new stone master to be a child."

"Who are you calling a child?" asked Wilf, rather upset.

"He must be talking to you, Wilf, because I'm definitely not a child, I'm three months older than you and I'll be growing facial hair in the next three years or so."

"Quiet!" shouted Liam. "Do you children ever listen?"

"Oooh!" said Wilf and Burp together. "Temper, temper!"

"If you are the stone master, then I fear that we are all doomed!" said Liam, shaking his head. "First we need food and heat to last the night. Wilf, take out the Orf stone."

"The what?"

"The stone that you ate."

"Oh, that Orf stone, I thought you were talking about another Orf st…"

"SHUT UP!" Wilf didn't try to finish his sentence; Liam might know lots of things, but how to laugh wasn't one of them.

The warrior took a deep breath, as if to say, "Right, we'll start again".

"Wilf, take out the Orf stone and hold it tightly in your hand. Now think of hot coals, then place the stone in front of you." Wilf looked at Liam.

"That's just what I need right now," he thought, "to be stuck with a nutter wearing a skirt!" But on balance he thought it better to do what was asked of him, so he took the stone from his pocket.

"How did that get there?" asked Burp. Liam gave him a frosty glare. "Er... tell me later," he decided, believing it unwise to upset a man who carried more weapons than a battleship.

Wilf took hold of the Orf stone; holding it tightly he thought of a roaring coal fire, then placed it in front of him. Soon the stone started to grow and change colour - the larger it grew the redder it became and finally, when it got to the size of a football, burst into flames.

"I bet you're glad you took that out of your pocket!" said Burp.

Liam, meanwhile, had gone down to the reservoir and collected some water in his shield. He also brought back two large rocks which he placed either side of the burning stone. Then, taking a small bag which had been tied to a strap round his waist, emptied its contents into the shield.

"Er... Liam, I hope you don't mind me asking, but just what are you doing?" enquired Burp.

"I am making us something to eat. This is called mull; not only is it good food, it is also warrior magic which will help you tomorrow."

"If you say so." Burp peered into the shield and screwed his face up, the way you would if you had just stood on a dog turd. "Urgh, it's green! Sorry, but I don't eat anything that looks like snot soup." Liam gave Burp another of his cold stares. Wilf also had a look in the shield.

"It's witches' brew. He's going to turn us both into toads!" grinned Wilf. Burp laughed.

"Yeah, hubble bubble toilet trouble."

"A couple of toads might be of more use," said Liam, sitting cross-legged between the two.

It was now dark but the stone gave off such warmth and light that the lads felt quite cosy.

"While we wait for the mull to cook we must talk." Liam's face was very serious. "I am sure that you would like to know why and how all these strange things have happened to you." Wilf shook his head.

"No, I'm not bothered, are you Burp?"

"Not really." Liam looked at Wilf, then Burp; he was very confused. The lads started to smile.

"Of course we'd like to know!" said Wilf. Liam was still very confused.

"I don't understand."

"Joke, Liam. You know, funny ha, ha!" Wilf tried to explain.

"Save your breath Wilf, this guy must have had his humour gland removed."

"So you *would* like to hear, then?" asked Liam.

"Good grief, YES!" shouted the lads. So the story began.

"In my world, many, many years ago, the Orf stone was used to heal people. The only person able to use it was the stone master as he alone had the power to read the words carved into it. It appears that you can use the stone, Wilf, because when you swallowed it your life-force caused it to activate. No one knew this could be done because no one has ever been stupid enough to swallow it before."

"Well, you were certainly stupid enough weren't you, Wilf?" said Burp.

"Yup, I sure was, young man."

"If you do not listen to me I shall have to gag you both!" Liam was starting to get angry again.

"I'm listening!" smiled Wilf.

"Me, too!" added Burp. Liam stared at the lads and wondered what he had done to be lumbered with two such idiots. He continued his story.

"The Orf stone also has the power to unlock the tomb of Tara where the cauldron of life is hidden. The cauldron of life is the power that keeps our worlds ordered and apart, which is why the banshee queen needs you.

71

"I don't understand why the banshee needs the stone or wants the power," said Burp.

"If you will let me, I will explain," replied Liam.

"Go ahead, young man, explain away." Liam went on.

"My world is made up of five lands: Bara - the people living here have great agility and are all great natural acrobats; Thoom - the people of this land have a great psychic ability allowing them to see into the minds of others; Bronac - the people here are blessed with great knowledge and like to invent and build; and Santra - the people here have great strength and this is where my family are from."

"Why did I know you were going to be from there!" said Wilf butting in.

"How did you know?" asked Liam, who had arm muscles like fully inflated footballs and a jaw that looked as though it had been carved from granite - if Arnold Schwarzenegger stood next to Liam he would seem like a wimp.

"Let's just say that I didn't think you were from Bronac," added Wilf. Liam, as usual, didn't understand so he just carried on with his story.

"Originally, the fifth land was uninhabited and known as the void since it contained nothing but marshes. None of the people from the various lands mixed, and this is how it was for centuries - until one day the banshees appeared. No one knows where they came from or why, but they arrived in their thousands and attacked each land. Even though the people of each land have a special gift they were no match for the banshees who would descend on the various cities screaming and wailing; the noise alone was enough to place a chill in the strongest of hearts. Some stood their ground and fought, others took to the hills. Those who fought were all killed - banshees do not take prisoners or show mercy.

Wilf and Burp were sat with their eyes wide open, like two small children having a bedtime story read.

"That's terrible! What happened to the people who hid?" enquired Burp.

"The survivors from each land realised that they could not beat the banshees without help, so their leaders met to discuss what should be done. Finally, it was agreed that each land should send a number of their strong young men to the void in order to share each other's skills and become a formidable army. These men became known as the marsh warriors, of which I am one."

"What happened then? Did you kick their butts?" asked Wilf eagerly.

"No. We were now inflicting losses on the banshees, but were also still suffering heavy losses ourselves," replied Liam. "We knew that the banshees were using some sort of power force, but we didn't know what it was. Then one day a band of our warriors came upon some banshees moving a cauldron."

"Was it the cauldron of life?" asked Burp, by now totally fascinated with the story.

"At first our warriors didn't give the cauldron a second thought, they just attacked the banshees and defeated all but one that seemed invincible after putting its hand into the cauldron. Our warriors were no match for it."

"Urggh... the thought of a banshee going wild and lashing out with those claws makes me feel weak just thinking about it," said Wilf, a shiver running down his back.

"Go on, tell us what happened next," urged Burp.

"One of our warriors had seen the banshee put its hand into the cauldron and believed that was where it had gained its power. So he managed to put his hand into the cauldron as well." As Liam spoke he started to get excited as if he too was living the story. His eyes had opened into a wild stare and he gave a menacing grin. Both lads were also caught up in the tale.

"Go on, go on!" they begged, eager to find out what happened next.

Liam could hardly contain himself. His face was alive with excitement and the glow from the Orf stone made him look as though he was sat in a shaded spot light. Jumping to his feet he drew his sword. The lads gasped with fear at the sight of the warrior with his huge, powerful body, holding the sword above his head, a murderous expression on his face. Liam started to speak in a loud, fast, excited voice.

"The warrior felt a power surge through his body, a power he had never felt the like of before. Shouting to the others he asked them to leave the banshee to him. The two came face to face.

"'So you have the power too?' snarled the banshee. 'How does it feel, monkey-man?'"

Liam was now doing all the actions with the story, wielding his sword around. Wilf and Burp moved back, neither wanting to get in the way. Liam carried on talking.

"The banshee lunged at the warrior who managed to step sideways, but long, razor-sharp claws caught his chest, cutting deep into his flesh. Yet the warrior felt no pain; he just

74

spun his sword and hit the banshee on the back of the neck, striking with such force that it didn't stand a chance. Letting out a blood-curdling scream it fell to the ground in a heap." Liam was now standing with the sword held triumphantly above his head.

"Phew!" gasped Burp, curled up on the floor.

"So your people captured the cauldron of life then defeated the banshees? asked Wilf.

"Yes," replied Liam as he stuck his sword back into the ground and sat down. "It was decided that the cauldron of life should be locked away in the tomb at Tara and the warrior became the first stone master."

"So how do you and the banshee queen fit into all this?" asked Wilf.

"This is the sad part," answered Liam. "All of the banshees were sent back to their own world using the cauldron. But it was agreed that the banshee queen was so dangerous it should be executed."

"Why? You could have sent it back with the rest of the banshees. After all, you had the cauldron so it couldn't come back," said Burp. Liam shook his head in disagreement.

"No, the queen had drunk from the cauldron giving it extra powers. Since no one knew just what it was capable of it had to die."

"I don't understand. If you killed the banshee queen, how come it was stood in front of me today?" asked Wilf. Liam dropped his gaze and stared at the floor with a look of bitter disappointment.

"The banshee queen was destroyed," he began, "and the warrior that had become the stone master used the magic of the Orf stone very well. He cured many people and our world returned to peace once more. Unfortunately, the warrior was just that - a warrior, trained to fight, and he had tasted the power of the cauldron. One day he sat thinking.

"'Just imagine the power and wealth I could bring to my world if I used the cauldron!'"

"You mean he got greedy?" asked Burp.

"No! Not greedy. He really thought that he could improve the lives of his people," snapped Liam.

"But your people had peace and the Orf stone made sure that there was no illness, so what more did they need?" asked Wilf.

"I don't know," replied Liam, still staring at the floor.

"So did the warrior use the Orf stone to get into the tomb?" asked Wilf.

"Yes."

"Well, go on then, tell us what happened," encouraged Burp, keen to hear the whole story. Liam let out a sigh; it was as if he didn't want to tell Wilf and Burp this part of the story, but he carried on.

"When the warrior went into the tomb he decided to drink from the cauldron to gain the full life-force. He certainly did this - you see the last person to drink from the cauldron had been the banshee queen, so that's the life-force he received."

"Oh, no! You mean it turned him into the banshee?" gasped Wilf in disbelief.

"Well, sort of. What it did was to join the warrior and the banshee together. The warrior was then trapped inside the banshee's body, making it one of the most powerful beings alive."

"Did it start the war all over again?" asked Burp.

"No. Before the banshee had time to get its revenge it mysteriously turned back into the warrior for a short while. Realising how stupid he had been the warrior told the Council of Elders what he had done. They realised that it was only a matter of time before he changed back into the banshee. So they took the Orf stone from him and locked him away in the Castle of Endless Time, where we first met, Wilf."

"WOW! What a story!" shouted Burp. Liam looked at him.

"It's not just a story. That's what really happened." Wilf was still a bit confused.

"So how come you were in the castle as well, then?"

"I was sent to guard the banshee and make sure that it never escaped." Burp started to laugh.

"I think you might be in for the sack when you get back to your world." Liam sighed again.

"I can never go back to my own world. My job now is to recapture the banshee."

"And what if you don't?" asked Wilf. Liam gave another of his cold stares.

"I *will* recapture it, even if it takes me until the end of time."

The lads didn't ask any more questions.

Liam took out three small bowls not much larger than egg-cups and filled them full of the liquid from the shield.

"Here, drink some mull," he offered, handing the lads a bowl each. Wilf looked at the green liquid.

"I don't think I can drink it."

"Why?" asked Liam.

"Because I feel scared."

"Me too," added Burp.

"What are you scared of?" asked Liam.

"I don't know, really. Maybe it's the thought of a big, hairy beast hunting me down. Or the fact that I'm stuck out here on the moors with a rather large, strange man who wears a skirt. Or perhaps I'm scared of talking to someone because there's a good chance they could turn into a beast and rip my head off! Maybe I'm just being silly!"

"And you've got a spot growing on the end of your nose," added Burp.

"Honest?" asked Wilf, trying to cover his nose.

"Honest. It's going to look like a small volcano by morning."

79

"Right, that's it, I've had enough!" shouted Wilf, jumping to his feet. "I'm going home!"

"You are not going anywhere!" snapped Liam angrily, grabbing Wilf's arm. Wilf's skinny little arm looked like a matchstick with Liam's huge hand round it. He knew that Liam would be strong, but hadn't realised just how much power the warrior had.

"Ouch! Get off my arm, you're going to break it, you idiot!" screamed Wilf. Liam let go.

"I am very sorry, I did not mean to cause you any pain," replied Liam.

"We can't stay here, our parents will be out of their minds with worry," said Wilf, rubbing his arm. "We should at least 'phone to let them know we're ok."

"I am sorry, but you cannot do that. The banshee will use those you love to get at you. Now please drink your mull, it will make you feel better."

"Why do I have to stay?" asked Burp.

"The banshee has seen you. It thinks that you are the one Wilf loves most, so you are in the most danger."

"GET LOST!" shouted Wilf. "I don't love him, he's my best mate, that's all. Can't that stupid banshee see that he's a boy? What does it think I am?" Liam and Burp watched in amazement as Wilf paced up and down, ranting and raving. "I've got a girlfriend, you know!" said Wilf, tapping himself on the chest as if to make a point. "Go on, Burp, tell him. Tell him about Molly." Wilf had, as they say, completely lost it. Burp thought this a good time to wind him up.

"How did the banshee find out our secret?" he asked with a straight face.

80

"WHAT SECRET?" screamed Wilf. "What are you talking about?"

"It's no good trying to deny it, Wilf, we must tell Liam about me and you, my love," replied Burp, trying hard not to laugh. Liam put his head in his hands and moaned.

"Please, will you two just stop this madness?!"

"It's easy for you not to be bothered, no one's saying that you fancy boys, are they?" said Wilf, pointing at Liam.

"Yeah, and you wear a skirt!" added Burp, just to keep the argument going.

"That's right," said Wilf, seizing on the point. "If I wore a skirt like you I could understand why the banshee would think I liked boys."

"I do *not* wear a skirt. This is a kilt!" replied Liam.

"It looks like a skirt to me. What do you think, Burp?"

"Yeah, my mum wears one like that. It's definitely a skirt," he answered, pleased that he'd managed to draw Liam into the stupid argument.

"Where I come from this is known as a kilt - it is the uniform of a warrior!" said Liam, feeling that he had to defend his dress sense.

"Well, where we come from it's known as a skirt and it's part of a schoolgirl's uniform." Burp couldn't take any more and burst out laughing. Wilf, realising his stupidity, also started to laugh. Liam, on the other hand, was still trying to explain that for thousands of years the marsh warriors had been proud to wear the kilt. It took him a few minutes of ranting and raving before he realised that the lads had been winding him up again.

"Here, just drink your mull," he said, handing the lads

one each of the little bowls. They looked at each other, smiling mischievously.

"Are you sulking?" Wilf asked Liam who sat stoney-faced.

"No, I'm just thinking."

"Well, it looks like a sulky think to me."

"I am not sulking!" shouted Liam.

"Ok, we believe you don't we, Burp?" smiled Wilf.

"No, I don't believe him." Liam jumped to his feet and walked away. He was so angry he was scared what he might do to the lads if they continued to wind him up so he went down to the reservoir for some peace and quiet. The lads stared at Liam's huge frame as he stood by the water, the moonlight making his shadow look like that of a strange tree.

"I don't know. They don't make marsh warriors like they used to!" laughed Burp.

"We'd better leave him alone for a while until he calms down," added Wilf. "There's no telling what he might do if he loses his temper."

"We must be mad, you know. I mean, we're out here all alone on the moors with a complete stranger." Burp was now starting to wonder just what the heck he was doing there. Wilf took a sup of his mull.

"I know, I've thought about that myself. If someone told me they were going to spend a night on the moors with a stranger I'd tell them not to be so stupid. But if they told me they were going to spend the night with a stranger who also carried more weapons than the American army, *and* wore a skirt, I'd have them put in a straight jacket and locked up!"

"So what are we doing here, then?" asked Burp, taking

a sup of his mull.

"I don't know. Today has been so strange that being here seems perfectly normal." Wilf finished off his drink. "You know, this stuff tastes quite nice," he said, pointing at his bowl. Burp finished his drink off and agreed.

"And it's very filling," added Burp. "I don't think I could drink another drop."

"Me neither." Liam had walked back from the side of the reservoir and was stood quietly behind them.

"We must stop this madness and talk." Both lads let out a scream, jumping up with fright. Liam drew his sword and prepared himself to fight, making the lads scream again. "What is it? What can you see that has frightened you?" asked Liam in a hushed voice, moving in circles with his sword held out in front of him. Wilf and Burp gasped a sigh of relief.

"Liam, will you please stop sneaking up behind us like that!" said Wilf putting his hand on his heart, just to check that it was still beating. Liam realised that he was responsible for the panic.

"It is no good, you are just children. We will need more help if we are to defeat the banshee," he said, sticking his sword back into the ground.

All three sat down round the Orf stone, quietly watching its bright red and orange flames flicker and dance in the cool summer night breeze. Suddenly, the silence was broken by Burp who let off the biggest fart this planet has ever heard.

"Good grief, I think my bum's just blown up!" said Burp, wafting his hand in front of his face to get rid of the smell. "What the heck is in that mull stuff? I've never let a fart off as big as that in my life!" The smell of it soon hit Wilf who

put his hands over his nose and gasped.

"BURP!! What have you been eating? It smells like something's crawled up your bum and died!!" Liam remained quiet, shaking his head.

"Have you any friends who may be able to help us?" asked Liam looking at them, tears running down their faces because of the smell. Liam didn't seem to be affected by it. "That was a stupid question, wasn't it?" he added.

"And what do you mean by that?" asked Burp, wiping away his tears. "We know lots of people don't we, Wilf?"

"That we do, young man," replied Wilf, nodding in agreement. Liam was amazed.

"You mean you two actually have lots of friends."

"I didn't say that," replied Burp, checking the back of his trousers just to make sure that the fart hadn't blown a hole in them. "What I said was that we knew lots of people."

"And would any of these people help if you were in trouble?" asked Liam, trying to keep his temper.

"No!" smiled Burp. Liam let out a sigh, the kind you let out when you find out that the person who pushed in front of you bought the winning raffle ticket.

"What about Knuckles and Snotty?" Wilf asked Burp. "They'd love a fight."

"That is very true, young man," replied Burp, "but they'd want to fight on the banshee's side."

"Yeah, you're probably right," agreed Wilf. "Anyway, the banshee's probably related to them. Good old Auntie Doris; she's very hairy but makes a wicked child stew." They both started to laugh, but Liam didn't.

"I think that we should get some sleep, it's going be

another long day tomorrow," he said, rising to his feet. Taking some of the herbs used to make the mull he sprinkled them in a circle around their camp. Wilf was about to ask him what he was doing when Burp put his hand over his mouth.

"Please don't ask, just go to sleep." Wilf smiled and nodded, then curled up in front of the Orf stone. Burp also huddled up and shut his eyes. Liam took his shield and laid it down to make a pillow, leaving his sword close by. He settled down, put his head on the shield and closed his eyes, leaving one hand over the hilt of his sword in case they had any unwelcome visitors.

There was a calm silence. All that could be heard was the rustle of the grass as the evening breeze snaked its way through the blades, leaving them shivering in the moonlight. Burp opened his eyes for a moment. He could see Wilf and Liam falling asleep. The glow of the Orf stone lit up half of their faces, the other half covered by the shadow of the night.

"Wilf, are you asleep yet?" whispered Burp.

"What?" Wilf whispered back, keeping his eyes tightly shut as he drifted to sleep.

"You know when you were in the hospital and the doctor told you to get back into bed?"

"Mmm," mumbled Wilf, too tired to talk.

"Well, as you climbed in your gown came open and everyone saw your bum!"

"'Night, Burp," replied Wilf, far too tired to care who had seen his bum.

"'Night, Wilf." With that, Burp shut his eyes and quickly fell into a deep sleep.

The sun rose over the Pennines as if it had just opened its eyes from a deep sleep, sending rays of light and warmth over the bracken-covered hills to reveal clusters of sheep, huddled together for warmth and safety during the night. The reservoir also lit up, sending out millions of little mirror lights as its surface gently bobbed and rippled in the summer morning breeze.

Wilf and Burp were still fast asleep, Liam was sat cleaning and sharpening his sword. On the Orf stone Liam's shield was filled with bubbling mull. Wilf slowly opened his eyes and tried to yawn but found that he couldn't since his tongue was stuck to the roof of his mouth. Burp was still fast asleep; his snoring sounded like someone cutting through a pipe with a hack-saw.

"Good morning!" said Liam to Wilf.

"Good morning," he replied, trying to prize his tongue from the roof of his mouth. It made a smacking noise and he looked like a lizard that had just eaten a big, fat cricket.

"There is some hot mull ready, take your bowl and fill it," said Liam, putting his sword back into its sheath.

"Thanks." Wilf filled his bowl and sat quietly sipping the mull, still feeling groggy from his night's sleep. He rubbed his eyes hoping that would help him see more clearly. His hair was sticking up and had bits of grass sprouting out, like the top of a pineapple. Wilf looked at Burp, laid on his back, mouth open, still fast asleep. He was making a growling noise like a small child does when pretending to be a lion.

"The last time I saw a mouth like that it had a hook in it," thought Wilf. Leaning over, he poured a small drop of mull into the open mouth. Burp was just in the process of breathing in when the mull hit the back of his throat. It felt as though someone had put a cork in his mouth and he jumped up, coughing and spluttering, holding his throat.

"What's wrong?" asked Wilf innocently.

"I think I've just swallowed a bug or something!" gasped Burp.

"Here, have a drink of mull, see if that'll clear it." Wilf handed his bowl to Burp.

"Here we go again!" thought Liam.

"That's better," said Burp after taking a gulp. "Thanks, Wilf."

"Don't mention it, young man," replied Wilf, feeling very pleased with himself.

After drinking their mull the two walked down to the reservoir and swilled their faces with the cold, refreshing water. Liam emptied the mull from his shield and wiped it clean.

While walking back Wilf turned to Burp.

"I've thought of two people who might help us."

"Who?" asked Burp, thinking that he might already

know the answer.

"Molly and Kirsty."

"That's amazing!" shouted Burp, his eyes wide open with surprise. "I was just thinking about them. Do you think that mull has given us the power to read each other's minds?" Wilf laughed and shook his head.

"No. I think it's because they're the only two people we know who'll talk to us." Burp thought for a second, then nodded.

"That is very true, young man, very true indeed."

On reaching Liam they found he was packed and ready to move. All that was left was the Orf stone, still burning brightly on the floor.

"You forgot to pack that," said Wilf, pointing to the stone.

"Only you can use the Orf stone."

"Ooh, that's going to hurt when you put it in your pocket!" cringed Burp. Liam gave Burp one of his cold stares.

"Wilf, place your hands round the stone and will it to return back to its original form," he said. Kneeling down, Wilf put his hands round the stone and thought back to what it had looked like previously. Slowly, it started to change colour and shrink, leaving the little stone bean that Wilf had swallowed the day before.

"How long should I leave it to cool down?" he asked.

"It will be quite cold now." Wilf touched the stone with his fore finger, then quickly pulled it away again.

"Yeah, it's cold." He picked up the stone and held it on his palm. "I think it might be safer if you kept the stone for a while," he said, offering it to Liam. This seemed to unnerve the warrior, who backed away.

"No, only you must keep the stone." The lads were surprised at the way Liam had reacted; it was as though he was scared of the stone.

"Ok, I'll look after it, but if I lose it don't blame me!" replied Wilf, popping the stone into his pocket. "We've thought of two people who might help us," he said, trying to change the subject.

"That is good. Who are they? Will they make great warriors?" Wilf smiled.

"They're called Molly and Kirsty. I don't know about making great warriors, but they certainly make great girlfriends!" Liam didn't like what he was hearing. He looked at Wilf in disbelief for a few seconds.

"They are females?" he asked in a quiet voice. Burp joined in the conversation.

"I hope so - one of them gave me a kiss!" Wilf was horrified.

"Which one kissed you?" he snapped, hoping that it wasn't Molly. Burp gave a cheeky grin.

"Kirsty." Wilf wasn't convinced.

"When?" he demanded.

"When they took you away in the ambulance."

"You mean I was laid out in the back of an ambulance, dying, while you snogged Kirsty? I'm glad I didn't spoil your day!" Wilf was starting to get upset again.

Burp thought for a moment; he didn't want to reveal that Kirsty had kissed him because he had been crying about Wilf. That would make him look soft.

"It wasn't like that."

"Well, what was it like then? snapped Wilf, believing that Burp couldn't have cared less how ill he'd been. "Was it, 'Well that's the end of Wilf, give us a snog to cheer me up Kirsty'?" Burp burst out laughing.

"Now you're just being stupid, Wilf. Me, Molly and Kirsty were so upset when they took you away that the girls started to cry." This brought a smile to Wilf's face.

"You mean Molly cried over me?"

"Yes." Wilf wanted to hear more.

"And then what?"

"Well, I asked Kirsty if she was ok and she just threw her arms round me crying, 'Oh, Burp,' then kissed me."

"Is that really what happened?" asked Wilf.

"Yeah, Scouts' honour," lied Burp, his fingers tightly crossed behind his back.

"You hate the Scouts," shouted Wilf, still not believing the story. Liam had had enough.

"Will you two stop this constant childish bickering?!" he shouted, taking a deep breath to calm himself down but still looking angry. The lads were worried. They had seen Liam's anger before, but never a laugh or a smile.

Then he gently placed his huge hand on Wilf's skinny shoulder. "Girls cannot be marsh warriors."

"That's sexist!" replied Wilf.

"What does sexist mean?"

"I don't know, it's just what my dad says whenever I say that girls can't do something," he replied with a feeble grin.

"Girls cannot, *should* not fight," added Liam. This maddened Burp.

93

"No one should fight, it's stupid."

"You would not fight to protect your land?" Liam asked Burp.

"I don't have any land." Wilf could see that Burp wanted to make a point. He could also see that Liam was starting to get angry again.

"I think what Burp is trying to say," offered Wilf, hoping to calm the situation down and stop Liam from squeezing his shoulder, "is that no one should want to take your land in the first place, because that too is stupid. In our world there are always wars because of ignorance and greed. It's always the innocent who suffer the most, never those who start the wars."

Burp couldn't believe that Wilf had just given such a speech. Neither could Wilf! The best speech he'd ever given before was when his teacher asked him to tell the class something that they might not already know. He then gave a brilliant speech on how to make a fart noise using a cupped hand and an armpit.

Liam was also impressed.

"I can see that the Orf stone is starting to give you great wisdom," he said, patting Wilf on the head as though he was a puppy.

"How can the Orf stone give me wisdom if it's no longer inside me?"

"You are now the stone master and so the power of the Orf stone will always be with you. As time passes you will learn to use this power. Let me show you how.

"Firstly, you must go back to school today. That's where you made the most wishes and so that is where the

94

banshee will look for you first. All the wishes you made yesterday will now have been broken; no one will remember a thing, so don't worry.

"Secondly, with the stone in your hand, you must tell your parents that you arrived home from school, and that you have set off to school this morning. Do the same for Burp."

Wilf took the Orf stone from his pocket. He conjured up a picture of his mum and dad in his mind and told them that he was ok. Then he did the same for Burp.

"Have you done that?"

"Yes," replied Wilf, opening his eyes.

"Good. Now you must remember that the banshee will take on someone else's life form, so you must trust no one."

"How will I know who the banshee is, then?" Liam gave Wilf a cold stare.

"You are the stone master; you will know."

"And what about me, how will I know?" asked Burp. Liam shook his head.

"The only way you will know is when the banshee has stayed in the life form too long and starts to lose its power. Then you will notice its eyes turn red."

"I once read a story about some witches with red eyes," said Burp.

Liam had turned his back on the lads and was starting to walk away.

"This is not a fairy story!" he shouted back, adding, "Don't worry; when the banshee appears I will be there to help. Now go to school." With that he vanished into thin air, leaving Wilf and Burp looking on in amazement.

"Neat trick!" said Burp. "I wish we could do that, it's going to take us ages to get to school." Wilf didn't answer; he was quietly thinking to himself. "What's wrong?" asked Burp. Wilf let out a sigh.

"If no one remembers anything about yesterday, then Molly and Kirsty won't be our friends anymore."

"We'll just have to make them remember, then," replied Burp.

"And just how will we do that?" Burp shrugged his shoulders.

"I don't know, you're supposed to be the stone master, you think of something." He looked at his watch. "We'll have to get a move on, school starts in ten minutes and it'll take us at least three hours to get there."

"No it won't!" said Wilf with some confidence. "We can get there instantly." Burp gave Wilf a puzzled look.

"Have you had a bump on the head that I don't know about?" Wilf laughed.

"We can use the life-force."

"Oh yes, the life-force, I forgot all about that!" mocked Burp. "Come on, let's find the nearest bus stop." He turned and set off walking. Wilf ran after him and grabbed his arm.

"Listen to me. Liam said that the banshee followed my life-force to get into our world. I think it uses the same thing to get about."

"So?" asked Burp, not understanding a word.

"Well, think about it, nugget head. If they can use my life-force, then why can't I?" Burp thought for a moment.

"Ok, what do we have to do?"

"I don't know," admitted Wilf, shrugging his shoulders.

"Goodbye, oh mystical one," said Burp, turning again and walking off. Then Wilf had an idea.

"Burp, wait! I think I know what to do!" he shouted. Burp stopped.

"This had better be good." Wilf took out the Orf stone and, holding it tightly in his hand, grabbed hold of Burp's arm.

"Now, shut your eyes and imagine that you're in the school playground." So they stood there, eyes shut, holding onto each other.

"This is stupid!" said Burp. "I'm glad that no one can see us."

"Look, just shut up and keep thinking - I'm sure it'll work," snapped Wilf.

"Well, I can't feel anything happening, can you?"

"And just what are you two idiots doing?" Both lads jumped.

"ARGHH!!" they screamed in fright and opened their eyes to see Molly.

97

"What are you doing here?" asked Burp. Molly shut her eyes and put her finger to the side of her head, as though she was deep in thought.

"Mmm, that's a tough question. Maybe it's because I go to this school, toad brain!" she shouted.

Wilf and Burp looked around and realised that they'd been standing in the middle of the playground, holding on to each other with their eyes shut. By now quite a crowd had gathered. They both felt so foolish that they wished the ground would open up and swallow them.

"Er... we were just practising our psychic powers," stuttered Wilf.

"You were just practising being a couple of nutters if you ask me!" said Molly, shaking her head as she walked away.

"Molly, come back!" shouted Wilf after her. Molly stopped and turned.

"What?" she snapped. Wilf didn't know what he was going to say, but he knew he had in some way to convince her that they'd been friends.

"I need to talk to you!" he blurted out.

"About what?" Wilf thought for a moment.

"Er... this is going to be difficult." But before he could say anything else Kirsty came walking across the playground.

"Hi, Molly!" she shouted, waving to her friend.

"Hi, Kirsty," said Burp with a big soppy grin on his face, forgetting that the girls couldn't remember a thing about the day before. Kirsty looked at Burp as though he was a dog turd.

"Drop dead, Dawson!" she snapped, her nose in the air.

"I suppose another kiss is out of the question, then?" sighed Burp under his breath, realising that she couldn't remember anything about the day before. Wilf grabbed Molly's arm.

"I need your help." Molly looked at Wilf's hand on her arm.

"I'm going to count to three. If you haven't removed your hand by then, I'm going to remove your teeth!"

"I wish Liam could hear you say that," thought Wilf, wisely moving his hand. "Look, what would you say if I told you that yesterday you and Kirsty became good friends with me and Burp," he said before Molly got chance to walk off again.

"I'd say goodbye, idiot! I've got better things to do." Molly turned and walked away, followed by Kirsty.

"You don't seem to be doing very well, young man," smiled Burp, not helping the situation. Wilf grabbed his arm.

"How much money have you got on you?" he snapped, shaking Burp.

"Why?" Burp pulled himself free.

"Quick, stop messing about and give me all your money."

"Is this a stick-up?" asked Burp, taking his money from his sock. Wilf did the same and counted it all up.

"Three pounds fifty, I just hope that's enough," he said, running after Molly and Kirsty.

"Molly, Kirsty, please stop for a minute!" shouted Wilf as he ran in front of them.

"Why don't you two creeps just bog off and leave us alone!" growled Kirsty. Wilf was out of breath as he'd just sprinted across the playground, so he took a deep breath.

"Look, I've got something to tell you, but it's so unbelievable that I don't even know if I believe it myself. Does that make any sense to you?" Molly laughed. She didn't know why, but in an instant she realised that she quite liked Wilf.

"Nothing you say makes any sense," she said with a huge, beaming smile which lit up her face and melted Wilf's heart.

"Ok, then. Here's three pounds fifty," he offered, unaware that he'd broken into his soppy grin again.

"What's that for?" asked Kirsty, wondering if Wilf was about to make a rude suggestion.

"You can keep that if you don't think what I'm going to show you is truly fantastic," replied Wilf. Kirsty grabbed Molly's arm and started to pull her away.

"Come on, Molly. I've heard stories about men like him."

"No, please listen! I promise you won't get hurt or anything horrible will happen."

"And we get to keep the three pounds fifty?"

101

"Yeah, honest."

"Eh… one pound fifty of that's mine!" cried Burp, not wanting to lose his money.

"Shut up!" shouted the others together. Then they all burst out laughing.

"Go on then, show us this fantastic thing - but I warn you, if it's rude you're dead!" said Molly, holding her fist up to Wilf. He quickly got out the Orf stone and held it out.

"Is that it? Is that the fantastic thing?" mocked Molly, pointing at the little stone bean in Wilf's hand. "Thanks for the three pounds fifty. 'Bye!" The girls linked arms and walked off, laughing.

"No, wait!" shouted Wilf after them. "I haven't shown you what it can do."

"Don't tell me, let me guess - it can grow into a huge beanstalk we can all climb up?" laughed Kirsty. Wilf thought for a moment.

"Actually it probably could do, but that isn't what I want to show you. How about going back to the museum we visited yesterday?" asked Wilf with a grin.

"If this is your strange way of asking me out on a date, forget it," laughed Molly. She didn't know why but she found the more she talked to Wilf the more she liked him. It was as if she'd been friends with him for years, but in truth neither Wilf nor Burp were the kind of lads the girls would own up to fancying.

"No, listen to me. Do you remember the room with the table covered with a green baize cloth?" pleaded Wilf.

"Yes," replied the girls.

"Well, we need to shut our eyes and hold hands and

102

think of that room."

"Why?" asked Kirsty. Wilf smiled.

"Because I bet I could show you the most fantastic thing you could see, and you two accepted my bet." The girls looked at each other, unsure whether to go along with this. After all, Wilf and Burp were well known for their stupid practical jokes.

"Ok," said Molly at last. "If we do this, will you leave us alone?"

"Scouts' honour" said Burp butting in. Wilf laughed.

"Ok then, let's all get into a circle and hold hands."

"Can I just ask one more question?" asked Kirsty.

"Yeah, sure," replied Wilf.

"Why does he keep looking at me like that?" she said, pointing her finger at Burp who was stood with misty eyes, his head to one side, hands clasped firmly together with the biggest soppy grin across his face as he stared lovingly at Kirsty.

"I'll soon sort that out for you," said Wilf, giving Burp a swift kick up the bum which brought him back to his senses. "Now, can we all hold hands and get this over with?" Burp glared at him.

The four gathered into a circle and shut their eyes, but Molly quickly opened hers again.

"I'm only holding hands for a minute, so don't get any funny ideas." They stood for a short while.

"Don't forget to think of that room in the museum," reminded Wilf, but Kirsty was already bored with all this silliness and opened her eyes. She started to speak but was struck with horror as she looked around.

"Right, that's it... ARGHH!!" she screamed. Molly

quickly opened her eyes thinking that the lads had played some sort of cruel trick. She was just about to ask what was wrong when she too realised where they were. Just a few seconds earlier they had been standing in the school playground but now they were in the museum.

"H... how d... did we get here?" stuttered Kirsty, clinging to Molly with fright.

"That's what I've been trying to tell you!" said Wilf as he jumped about, so pleased his plan had worked. "It's the Orf stone - it has magical powers, and only I can use them. It's fantastic, isn't it?"

"Yes, yes, it's fantastic. Now please, just get us back to school!" begged Molly.

"Ok, then. Get back into a circle, hold hands, and think of the school playground," said Wilf, feeling more than a little pleased with himself.

Meanwhile, a security guard who had been watching the monitors in the museum saw four children suddenly appear from nowhere. He jumped back in his chair with fright, then hit the alarm button before running out to try and catch what he thought were burglars.

"Right, we can open our eyes again now," said Wilf. Burp opened his eyes first but didn't want to let go of Kirsty's hand. It felt so soft and warm; he'd never held hands with a girl before.

The girls slowly opened just one eye, afraid they might be somewhere else instead of back at school, but they had no need to worry; as they looked around they could see the familiar suroundings of the school playground.

The four stood for a while, still holding hands, Wilf

104

and Burp with huge smiles on their faces, Molly and Kirsty with horror on theirs.

Back at the museum the red-faced security guard was telling police that he'd definitely seen four children holding hands.

Wilf and Burp started to tell Molly and Kirsty all about the day before: how Knuckles and Snotty had been scared of them; how old Thomas's hair had flapped up and down as he spoke - the girls fell about laughing. If they hadn't witnessed the power of the Orf stone for themselves they would never have believed such amazing stories, but now they were willing to believe anything the lads told them.

Wilf described how the Orf stone had made him ill and he'd been taken to hospital.

"You two started to cry, and Kirsty even gave Burp a hug and kiss because she was so upset, didn't she, Burp?" said Wilf, trying to catch his friend out. Burp could feel his face starting to tingle with heat as he blushed bright red.

"Er... something like that, yeah," he mumbled.

"UGHH!! I never did!" said Kirsty, rubbing her lips as if to wash the kiss off. Burp quickly picked up the story, hoping it would make her forget what Wilf had just said. He told them all about the banshee queen and Liam, and how they had spent a night on the moors.

Wilf butted in describing how Liam had asked them

107

to get help, which was why they had to prove what they were saying was true.

"Wait a minute!" said Molly, frowning. "Did you wish for us to be your girlfriends?" Wilf and Burp looked at each other; both were squirming with embarrassment.

"Did we heck!" replied Wilf with a half-hearted laugh.

"Yeah, what do you think we are?" added Burp, hoping the girls wouldn't find out the truth.

"I'm sorry," said Molly. "I should've known that even you two wouldn't be that sad." The lads looked at each other and cringed; after all, they really were that sad.

"So what you're trying to say is that you'd like me and Kirsty to help you," asked Molly.

"Got it in one," replied Wilf.

"No thanks, it sounds too dangerous to me."

"Me, too!" added Kirsty.

"So you won't help us then?" asked Burp, shocked; he'd taken it for granted that they would.

"You're very quick at understanding things, you know," said Kirsty, mocking Burp.

But Wilf wasn't going to give up that easily; he knew the best way to get them on their side. He took hold of Burp's arm.

"Come on, Burp, Liam was right, we should never have asked a couple of girls to help us."

"And just what do you mean by that?" snapped Molly, falling into Wilf's trap. He looked at the girls as though he didn't care anymore.

"Well, Liam said that girls could never become marsh warriors because they're not bright or brave enough."

"What rubbish!" shouted Kirsty.

"Yeah, we're more than a match for any boy!" added Molly.

"That's what I told Liam, but he didn't believe me. I suppose he'll say, 'I told you so' when he finds out you won't help."

"We won't help because we're not daft enough to put ourselves in danger!" snapped Kirsty, growing angry. Burp realised what Wilf was trying to do.

"What you said was that it was too dangerous, and you're right, it is. We're sorry we asked. Anyway, we'd better get off now and find two lads to help us, like Liam said." With that Wilf and Burp walked away.

Molly and Kirsty weren't going to let them get away, so they ran after the lads. Molly caught hold of Wilf by his t-shirt and forcefully swung him round.

"You can't ask people to help you then just take it back!" she shouted. Wilf stared at Molly, puzzled.

"But you don't want to help."

"Well we've changed our minds, haven't we, Molly?"

"Yes, we have!" Molly agreed.

"Are you sure? I wouldn't want to talk you into something you didn't want to do." Molly and Kirsty were pleased that they were making a point.

"Just tell us what we have to do." Wilf smiled.

"I don't know what we're supposed to do. We were just told to get help and wait for the banshee to find us."

"What will the banshee look like, then?" asked Molly.

"When you see a banshee in its true form you'll know you're looking at one, believe me! But they're shape-shifters

109

which means they can take on any life form, so it could look like anyone. The only way you can tell is when it starts to lose its powers as the whites of its eyes will turn red," explained Wilf.

"I once read a story about some witches whose eyes were..."

"We know, we know!" said Burp, stopping Kirsty from telling the story. "But this isn't a story," he added, repeating what Liam had said to him when he tried to tell the same story.

"So what do we do if we find this banshee?" asked Kirsty. Wilf shrugged his shoulders.

"I don't know. I hope Liam will turn up and sort it."

Molly folded her arms looking very confused. Glancing at Wilf she opened her mouth as if to speak but then stopped. Finally, she spoke.

"So you want us to sit back and let the banshee come to us? And when, if, it does, we won't recognise it? And if we do recognise it you want us to sit back and do nothing?" Wilf looked at Burp to get some support, but he just shrugged his shoulders.

"Er... yeah, I suppose so," he replied, knowing that it sounded stupid.

"So you don't want us to do anything really," added Kirsty. Wilf didn't know what to say; Kirsty was right, he didn't know why Liam had told him to get help, or what he was supposed to do.

"I think that when the banshee appears we'll all know what to do," said Burp, trying to help Wilf out.

"I think we should get into school now, we're already

late," said Wilf before the girls could ask any more questions. They all agreed and set off.

The lads went to the locker room to get their pens out of their coats where they'd left them the day before, while Molly and Kirsty went straight to their class-room.

In the locker room there were still quite a few children, also late. Some were shouting, others chatting, while the rest were swopping various objects. This is how it always was in the locker room.

Burp asked Wilf if he was scared. After all, they didn't know what was going to happen that day.

"I feel really calm. I think it must be that mull we drunk."

"Yeah, me too," agreed Burp. "You never did tell me how you got the Orf stone out." Wilf laughed.

"It was simple. Liam told me to wish it out and it just appeared in my hand."

"OI DAWSON, 'ANG MI COAT UP FER MI!"

Wilf and Burp had no need to turn round to see who the voice belonged to - every kid in the school recognised Knuckles's tough, yobbish voice, the one he used to terrorise the other children.

Burp slowly turned to face Knuckles, knowing the wish had worn off and that the bully was no longer scared of him. But strangely, Burp was no longer scared of the bully. He sneered at Knuckles then spoke in a very loud, slow voice, just to make sure everyone could hear.

"DROP DEAD, CREEP!"

The locker room fell silent. The others stood motionless, their mouths hung open in disbelief. Those who

111

couldn't stand the sight of blood shut their eyes, afraid of what might happen next. Even Knuckles couldn't believe what he'd heard, so went to level two of bullying – inflate your chest and snarl at your victim.

"WOT DID YER SAY?!" snarled Knuckles. Wilf shut his eyes for a second.

"Oh, no! Here we go again," he thought. "Burp has to make a point." Burp, on the other hand, was starting to enjoy himself. He sneered at Knuckles a second time, knowing that this would really wind him up.

"I SAID D.R.O.P. D.E.A.D., C.R.E.E.P.!" he repeated in a slow, loud voice, spelling out the words as he said them.

Knuckles was dumb-struck for a second, then realised that he would have to go to level three of bullying - make yourself look as big as possible then stick your face menacingly into the face of your victim.

So Knuckles stomped over to his victim. He stood head and shoulders above Burp and leaned forward, pressing his nose tightly into Burp's face.

"Say that again!" he commanded in a low, growling voice. Burp just pushed him back, wafting his hand in front of his face.

"Phew! Have you brushed your teeth today?" The silence in the locker room was now deafening. Some of the other children were too frightened to even breathe. It was then that Knuckles realised he would have to go to level four of bullying.

Now in the bullies' handbook, entitled *How to Make Someone's Life Unbearable*, it states that a bully should only go to level four if: (a) he is with a group of bullies; (b) he has a sidekick resembling a gorilla; (c) the victim is far smaller and weaker because level four involves physical violence. This begins with the victim's arm being twisted into a position it is clearly not meant to be in, ending with the victim losing teeth, money or having his head shoved down the toilet, whichever happens to be most convenient for the bully. Luckily for Knuckles, Burp fell into category (c).

However, before Knuckles could make his move, Wilf stepped forward.

"Just what is your problem, Parker? Why do you always have to harass and beat people?" Knuckles was starting to panic. No one had ever stood up to him before.

"I'll have to see it through," he thought. "There might be two of them, but they're only half my size."

There was a stand-off for a few seconds as Knuckles eye-balled Wilf and Burp, hoping they would back down. There was silence all around. Then, from the back of the room, came a small voice.

"Why do you always nick my dinner money? I had to go without my dinner three times last week." It was one of the first years, a small, thin boy with bright, frizzy, ginger hair. His face was covered with freckles and he wore thick, black-rimmed glasses. Everyone turned to look at him and he went bright red, wondering what the heck had made him say that.

But then one of the second year girls chipped in.

"Yeah, why don't you ever pick on someone your own size?"

"Because he's a coward!" shouted another girl.

One by one all the children joined in. They shouted

113

the things that they'd always wanted to say to the bully but had been too frightened to. For the first time in his life Knuckles panicked - now *he* knew what it felt like to be picked on. He felt so helpless, but unlike the children he'd tormented over the years, Knuckles didn't have the courage to face the problem. So he did what all cowards do in this situation - he turned and ran.

The locker room erupted with cheering and shouting and the children started to dance about as if they had just scored the winning goal in the World Cup. Everyone kept slapping Wilf and Burp on the back and said how brave they were. Little did they know that if Burp hadn't drunk the mull earlier on he *would* have hung Knuckles's coat up for him.

The two pushed through the crowd and went to their class-room. Molly and Kirsty were already sat at their desks and waved to the lads as they came in. Miss Dennis hadn't arrived yet so there was a lot of shouting and people throwing things about. Then Miss Williams, the secretary, walked in.

"WHAT ON EARTH IS GOING ON IN HERE?" she shrieked. The class fell silent as Miss Williams peered at them over her horn-rimmed specs.

"Miss Dennis is going to be a little late this morning, so I'll sit with you for a while," she hissed. "Oh, yes. Wilf Sexton, Mr Thomas would like to see you in his office. Urgently!"

Wilf's heart started to race; what could old Thomas want him for? He knew that the Head wouldn't be able to remember what had happened the day before, and he couldn't think of anything else he'd done wrong – well, not this week anyway. He turned to Burp.

114

"I think this is it - old Thomas must be the banshee!" Burp felt a shiver run down his spine.

"I'll come with you," he said, afraid of what might happen to his friend. Molly leaned over and asked Wilf what he'd done wrong.

"Nothing," he replied. Molly let out a gasp as she realised that this could be a trap.

"Do you think it could be the banshee?" she asked. Wilf nodded slowly and, taking the Orf stone from his pocket, handed it to Burp.

"If this is a trap and Liam doesn't get here the banshee won't kill me until it has the Orf stone. If you keep hold of it we might be able to buy a bit of time."

"But you'll need it to fight the banshee," said Burp. Wilf stood up.

"I don't know how to use its powers properly, so I think it's best to do it this way until Liam gets here," he said and walked out of the class-room.

"Good luck!" shouted Molly and Kirsty after Wilf as they crossed their fingers and held them up for him to see.

Outside, Wilf walked nervously down the long corridor. His heart was beating so fast and loud that he was sure the people passing by could hear. Finally, he arrived outside the door with the sign saying "THE HEAD".

"This is it!" he thought, wiping his hands down his t-shirt as he sweated. Then, taking a deep breath, he knocked quietly on the door.

"ENTER!" boomed the loud, theatrical voice from the other side.

"It certainly sounds like old Thomas," thought Wilf to himself. He opened the door nervously and put his head round, just in case there were any surprises awaiting him.

"Ah, Wilf, young man. Come in, come in and sit down." Now this was strange. Mr Thomas had dropped the usual theatrical voice for a more caring one; and he was being nice. Wilf was worried; he, and every other child in the school, knew that one of Mr Thomas's golden rules was never to be nice to children.

He tried to walk towards Mr Thomas but found his legs had turned to jelly. His stomach had a tight knot inside it and his body was shaking so much that as he walked it looked as though he'd had all his bones removed. Mr Thomas noticed Wilf's strange behaviour.

"Don't be afraid, boy, I'm not going to eat you!"

"Why did he say that?" wondered Wilf. It seemed such a strange thing to say. The lad sat in the chair and peered across the desk at Mr Thomas who began to smile. "I didn't know that he could smile," thought Wilf. First old Thomas had been nice, then smiled; surely this couldn't be the real Mr Thomas? Then, dropping the smile, he slowly leaned forward over his desk.

"I'm afraid that I have some rather bad news for you, young man," he said quietly.

"That's it!" thought Wilf. "He's going to pounce on me!" Jumping quickly to his feet he picked up the chair he'd been sat on. "Get back, you creep, I know who you really are!" he shouted. Mr Thomas jumped back in horror, then got to his feet.

"What on earth is wrong, boy? What are you talking about?"

"You don't fool me!" replied Wilf. "I know you're the banshee! Come on, let's see you for what you really are!" Wilf hadn't realised just how heavy the chair was and was having difficulty hold it up. Mr Thomas held his arms out to protect himself as the lad wobbled round the room, desperately trying to keep the chair up.

"Put the chair down, boy. I was only going to tell you that your mother has had an accident and been taken into hospital."

"What?" screamed Wilf. "What have you done to her?"

118

"For God's sake, boy, I haven't done anything to her! We received a 'phone call from the hospital a short while ago saying that your mother had been involved in an accident and you were needed at the hospital." The look on Mr Thomas's face told Wilf that he wasn't lying and he suddenly felt very foolish as he lowered the chair to the floor. "Good grief, young man, what has got into you?"

"Er… sorry, Sir, I thought you were someone else," mumbled Wilf, turning bright red.

There was a knock on the door.

"ENTER!" boomed Mr Thomas using his more usual theatrical voice. In walked Mr Howe, Wilf's favourite teacher. He was a large man with black, curly hair who looked more like a boxer than a teacher but had a great sense of humour and always treated everyone fairly, unless you tried to mess him about. Then he'd let you know you'd just picked on the wrong person.

"Mr Howe is going to take you to the hospital," said Mr Thomas. "Unless you think he's a banshee as well!" he added. Wilf looked at Mr Howe and smiled, but knew there was a possibility he could be the beast. After all, wouldn't it be easier for the banshee to catch him if it was disguised as someone he trusted? But then he remembered what Liam had said about knowing the banshee when he came face to face with it, and Mr Howe seemed ok.

"Now go on, get off to the hospital," said Mr Thomas, "but I want to see you when you get back regarding that stupid outburst a minute ago."

"Ok, Sir." Wilf and Mr Howe left the office. Once outside Wilf said he'd better go back to his class to tell Miss

Williams what was happening.

"Ok, but try to be quick. I'll wait for you in my car outside the school gates." Wilf ran off down the corridor to his class.

When he walked back into his class-room Burp, Molly and Kirsty smiled with relief; Wilf was ok. He told Miss Williams that he had to go to the hospital then went to his desk, pretending to pick something up. He whispered to Burp.

"Old Thomas is definitely not the banshee but I think he might act like one when I get back!"

"Why?"

"It's a long story, I'll tell you later." Then he quickly told Burp about his mum's accident.

"That's terrible!" gasped Burp. "Do you think it could've been the banshee?"

"I hope not. If it was, then it's my fault." Burp asked how he was getting to the hospital and Wilf said Mr Howe was waiting outside for him in his car.

"Can you trust him?"

"I think so, but I've got a feeling that something bad's about to happen. Oh, where's Liam? I feel that we're all in great danger." Burp could see that Wilf was shaken and worried.

"Do you want the Orf stone back? You might be able to use it to help your mum."

"No, this might be a trap. Keep it until Liam gets here, but whatever you do, don't let anyone know you've got it." Before Wilf could say any more Miss Williams shouted.

"Sexton, if you're going to the hospital, get off and leave Dawson to get on with his work!" Wilf gave Burp a smile; he didn't know why but he felt as though he might never see him again. Burp smiled back; he had the same feeling, and held out his hand.

"'Bye mate. And good luck!" Wilf was overcome with emotion - his mum was in hospital and now he could lose his best friend. A lump came to his throat and tears started to fill his eyes. Wilf took a deep breath and swallowed; the last thing he wanted to do was cry in front of his class-mates. He shook Burp's hand.

"Yeah, the same to you pal." Wilf turned to walk away but suddenly looked back at his friend.

"Give me one of your best ones before I go." Burp smiled. Taking a deep breath he swallowed and then, forcing air through the back of his throat, produced a humungous burp, one that any bullfrog would have been proud of. Wilf laughed. "Pure poetry, young man, pure poetry."

"Dawson, was that you?" shouted Miss Williams. Burp winked at Wilf.

"Yes, Miss, sorry. I seem to have a bit of breakfast trouble this morning." Wilf waved goodbye to Molly and Kirsty and went, leaving Miss Williams struggling to stop the rest of the class from laughing.

Wilf wiped his eyes as he walked to the entrance and down the drive. Looking back at the building he kept asking himself the same question.

"Why do I feel like this?" Then an awful thought struck him like a bolt of lightning, sending a shock through his body that stopped him dead in his tracks. Was this the feeling Liam had told him about? Was Mr Howe the banshee?

Wilf could see the teacher sat in his car, waving at him to get a move on. Suddenly, Wilf's body started to shake and he could feel his mouth getting dry. He walked slowly towards the car, all the time staring straight at Mr Howe, searching for any sign that he was the banshee. There didn't seem to be anything different about him, but then there wouldn't be unless the banshee was losing its powers.

Wilf drew nearer to the car. Should he get in? Mr Howe put his head out of the window.

"Come on, Wilf, get a move on!" Wilf knew that he had to draw the banshee out, and trusted Liam to turn up at the right moment. So the boy opened the car door and took another look at Mr Howe, still checking for any telltale signs that he was the banshee. Mr Howe smiled at Wilf, ashen with fear.

"Don't worry, Wilf, I'm sure your mum will be ok. Now get in, I'll have you at the hospital in no time," he said reassuringly. Wilf climbed in, not once taking his eyes off Mr Howe.

"What's wrong, Wilf? I'm not going to bite you you know!" said Mr Howe with a laugh. Little did he know that that was just what Wilf was scared of!

As they set off Wilf sat in silence, glancing out of the corner of his eye at Mr Howe. Slowly, he realised that the horrible feeling was not about Mr Howe, or even about himself being in danger, but was for Burp's safety. He could feel something terrible was about to happen to his friend, but didn't know what.

Back in the class-room, Burp leaned over to Molly and Kirsty's desk while Miss Williams was busy reading. He told them in a whisper all that Wilf had said.

"That's terrible!" whispered Molly. "Do you think it could've been the banshee that got her?"

"I don't kn... Ouch!!" screamed Burp, suddenly hoisted out of his chair by his ear. He was spun round and came face to face with the sharp features of Miss Williams.

"Would you like to tell us all what is so interesting, boy?" she hissed. Burp could smell garlic on her breath as she pushed her hideous face close to his.

"Nothing, Miss!" gasped Burp, wriggling about in an attempt to free his ear so he didn't die of garlic poisoning.

"But I've just seen you talking when you should have been writing," she hissed, the odour of garlic and tiny bits of spit spraying Burp like an aerosol. He winced, more from the smell of her breath than the pain in his ear. Then he saw it.

"Oh, no!" he thought. "Why didn't I notice that before?" It was Miss Williams's right eye - it was turning red! He also noticed deep lines under her eyes and down her cheeks

123

that he'd never seen before which she'd tried to cover up by plastering on lots of make-up. This made her look like one of the ugly sisters from a Cinderella pantomime.

"This is it!" thought Burp. "Miss Williams is the banshee. I must do something!" So he did the first thing that came into his head which was to push her as hard as he could.

Miss Williams fell backwards, her legs buckled like two thin bows. Then she actually fell off her high heels and over Burp's desk, letting out a high-pitched scream as she hit the floor, legs up in the air. Her tight skirt had ridden up to reveal a pair of heart-covered pink frilly knickers which she wore over her black tights.

"Assault! Assault!" she screamed repeatedly with high-pitched wailing. Burp picked up his chair and held it out as though he was a lion-tamer.

"She's the banshee!" he shouted to Molly and Kirsty. "Look at her eyes!" The girls ran over and peered at Miss Williams, sprawled out on the floor, screaming.

"You're right!" they gasped seeing her right eye, now bloodshot. The rest of the class, silent at first from shock, were now laughing and screaming at the sight of Burp with the chair and Miss Williams showing her knickers. Molly turned to them.

"Everyone get out of the class-room - you're all in great danger!" This just made them laugh even more; they thought it was great fun and that Molly, Kirsty and Burp had gone completely mad.

Miss Williams, meanwhile, was still lying with her legs in the air.

"Assault! Assault!" she screamed.

124

"Shut up, you old hag, you don't fool me!" snarled Burp, pushing the chair forward at her but rather surprised at the banshee's lack of action. He never thought that when he came face to face with the banshee it would just lay there with its legs in the air showing him its knickers! Although the sight of Miss Williams's knickers was a bit scary, it was hardly frightening.

Miss Williams's high-pitched screams had not gone unnoticed; Mr Thomas could hear them from his office and stormed into the class-room to see what was wrong. He couldn't believe the sight that greeted him: Burp with the chair, Molly and Kirsty trying to get the class to leave the room, the class cheering and laughing and poor old Miss Williams showing her knickers to anyone wanting a look.

"What on earth going on in here?" he boomed. The class fell silent except for Miss Williams's screams.

"I thought I'd told you to shut up, you old hag!" snarled Burp again at a tearful Miss Williams.

"Dawson, put that chair down now, boy!" commanded Mr Thomas.

"I can't, Sir, you don't understand." Burp was trying to think of some way to explain what he was doing but decided the truth was the only way. He pushed the chair into Miss Williams's beak-like nose, just to make sure that she didn't try anything funny.

"She's not who she seems to be, Sir. You think this is Miss Williams, the school secretary, when really she's a seven foot high, hairy banshee." The rest of the class put their hands over their mouths to stop themselves from laughing at what seemed to be the most stupid statement most of them had

125

ever heard. Some even rolled their jumpers up to bite on they thought this so funny.

Kirsty jumped to Burp's defence.

"It's true! It might sound stupid, but it's true!" she shouted. Then Molly joined in.

"Look at her right eye... it's turning red. When the banshee starts to lose its powers its eyes go red."

"I've had enough of this nonsense!" boomed Mr Thomas. He marched over to Burp and, snatching the chair from his hands, sent him flying across the room. Miss Williams jumped to her feet, adjusted her skirt and ran out of the room screaming and waving her arms in the air, leaving behind her white high-heeled shoes which had fallen off earlier.

"Sir, we have to stop her. Look at her eyes - she's a banshee!" pleaded Burp. Mr Thomas grabbed hold of Burp by the scruff of his neck and dragged him across the room.

"You two, to my office. Now!" he snapped, turning to Kirsty and Molly. "The rest of you carry on with your work until Miss Dennis arrives. Any noise and you will all be on detention." He dragged Burp out of the class-room and on to his office.

Wilf and Mr Howe arrived at the hospital and went through the huge automatic doors into the main entrance.

"I hope my mum's ok!" Wilf kept thinking to himself over and over again. He was still worrying about the feeling he had that Burp was in serious trouble. Little did he know that Burp *was* in serious trouble, but not the kind he thought. He couldn't help but worry that people were starting to get hurt, and it was all his fault. "If I hadn't swallowed that stupid stone in the first place, none of this would have happened," he decided.

Mr Howe put his hand gently on Wilf's shoulder.

"Come on, we'll go to reception and see if they can find your mum for us." They went over to the desk Burp had gone to the day before to enquire about Wilf and there was the same grumpy old man, still sorting out the mail.

Mr Howe pressed the buzzer on the side of the desk. The old man looked up, saw Mr Howe and immediately put down the mail. It seemed that adults were far more important to him than children.

"Yes, Sir, how can I help you?" he smiled, far more

pleasant with adults than he was with children.

"We're looking for Mrs sexton. I believe she was involved in an accident and brought in this morning."

"Can I have her first name, please?" asked the old man politely. Mr Howe looked at Wilf for help.

"Her first name's Carol. Carol Sexton." The old man started to punch away on the keys of his computer in front of him.

"I'm sorry," he said a couple of minutes later, "but I can't find anyone by that name in the hospital."

"Are you sure?" asked Mr Howe.

"I'm quite sure," replied the old man.

"But the hospital 'phoned my school to tell me to get here quick because my mum had had an accident," said Wilf, very confused.

"And you are?" enquired the old man.

"I'm Wilf Sexton, her son." The old man turned to Mr Howe.

"So you must be Mr Sexton."

"No, my name is Howe, I'm Wilf's teacher." The old man smiled, clasped his hands together and leaned on the desk.

"Well, Sir," he said with a smug grin, "don't you think that if this woman had been involved in an accident we would have 'phoned her husband, not her child?" Mr Howe was confused but had to admit the old man did have a point.

"Come on, Wilf, it seems as though we've been the victims of a cruel hoax." He thanked the old man for his help, but Wilf didn't want to leave.

"I'm still worried about my mum, Sir."

"I can understand that. Look, there's only one way to sort this out. Where would your mum normally be this morning?" Wilf thought for a moment.

"It's her day off, Sir, she should be at home." Mr Howe smiled.

"Well then, why don't we 'phone her to see if she's ok."

"Sir, has anyone ever told you you're a genius!" laughed Wilf.

"Oh, many times Wilf, many times," lied Mr Howe. Wilf hurried into the 'phone box in the main entrance. He shuffled around for a minute then rather sheepishly came back out.

"Er... you couldn't lend us ten pence could you, Sir?" asked Wilf, realising Molly still had his money. Mr Howe laughed and handed him a coin.

"That's ten pence you owe me, so don't leave the country." Wilf ran back to the 'phone box and dialled his home number. He could hear the tone ringing as he waited what seemed like hours.

"Please, mum, pick up the 'phone," he said to himself over and over again. Suddenly, there was a voice on the other end.

"Hello."

"Mum! Is that you?!" It seemed like weeks since he'd heard his mother's voice, though in fact it was only yesterday. Of course, she didn't know that Wilf hadn't been home; as far as she was concerned she'd waved him off to school that morning. "Oh, mum! Someone 'phoned school and told me you'd been in an accident and were in hospital, so Mr Howe ran me up here," Wilf blurted out, nearly in tears at the relief of finding out his mum was ok.

"What a sick trick!" replied his mum. "But I assure you I'm ok, love. Would you like to come home?" It was then that Wilf realised what was happening; this was all just a set-up to get him out of the way. Could his mum be the banshee?

"Oh, no! The banshee's after Burp!" he thought. "Mum, I'm going back to school," said Wilf quickly.

"Ok then, love, but I'll call into school later on to see if I can sort all this out." Wilf was just about to say goodbye when a thought struck him.

"What if this is mum? I might not see her again if the banshee gets me!" So he said something that he hadn't said in a long time. "Mum?"

"Yes, love?" replied his mum, concerned at the serious tone of his voice.

"I love you, mum." There was silence for a second from the other end of the 'phone as Wilf's mum choked back tears on hearing those words her son hadn't said for a long, long time.

"I love you too, son," she said softly. Wilf said goodbye and put the 'phone down, feeling as though one weight had been lifted off his shoulders only to be replaced by another.

He now knew for certain that the banshee was after Burp, and maybe Molly and Kirsty too. He wanted Mr Howe to help, but how could he get him to believe such a ridiculous story. After all, would you believe someone if they'd just told you that a seven foot high, hairy banshee was trying to kill their best friend?

Wilf thought that it might be better to make up a

story and try to explain things later. He ran from the 'phone box over to Mr Howe.

"Sir, I think I know who made the 'phone call. We have to get back to school quick because Burp Dawson's in danger." Mr Howe was shocked.

"What are you talking about? What's wrong?" he asked.

"Sir, this morning, when we were going to school, a crazy bloke started to threaten us saying that if we didn't go with him he would kill me and Burp and our families. I think he might be at school now!" lied Wilf.

"Why didn't you say anything about this before?" Wilf didn't like having to lie like this, but knew it was his only chance to help Burp.

"We just thought he was a nutter, Sir, so we ran off. I never gave it another thought until now." Mr Howe told Wilf to stay where he was, then went to the 'phone box and rang school. He waited and waited, but there was no reply. Mr Howe was worried; Miss Williams was always quick to answer the 'phone. Little did he know that Miss Williams was actually sat on the toilet crying, her thick, black mascara smudged all over her eyes making her look like an under-fed, beaky panda.

Mr Howe ran back out of the 'phone box and called Wilf over.

"Come on, I think we should get back to school as quickly as possible." Wilf followed Mr Howe out of the hospital. He was half hoping that Burp was in some sort of trouble because if he wasn't, Wilf certainly was.

Back in Mr Thomas's office Burp, Molly and Kirsty were stood in front of the Head, out of breath after dragging Burp along the corridor. His hair, usually worn like a piecrust, had fallen down over his eyes like long, thin spider's legs. Burp and the girls knew they were about to receive a serious telling-off, when old Thomas got his breath back. Finally he'd gasped enough air to speak.

"Now, do please tell me what on earth you thought you were doing back there?"

"I know this sounds silly, Sir," said Burp, "but we believe that Miss Williams is really a banshee!"

"Have you been taking drugs, Dawson?" boomed old Thomas.

"Not as far as I know, Sir," replied Burp.

"Don't be cheeky, boy!" he snarled.

"It's true, Sir, there are things happening that you don't understand," added Molly.

"And what would you say if I told you that someone attacked me with a chair and accused me of being a banshee only this morning?" Burp had to stifle his laughter at this news.

"I'd say that I think I know who that was, Sir."

"But you must believe us, Sir, Miss Williams is a banshee!" added Kirsty. "She had a red eye."

"I know she had a red eye," replied Mr Thomas. "I helped to remove a hair from it this morning, although how it got there is a mystery."

"Oh, dear!" thought Burp. It all made sense now. Miss Williams would have got the hair in her eye when she was trying to stop old Thomas's hair from flapping up and down the day before. And if she had been the banshee, Burp and his chair would never have stopped it.

The girls, too, had worked out their mistake from what Wilf and Burp had told them earlier.

They all looked at each other, knowing they were now in serious trouble.

"Er... there could have been a slight case of mistaken identity here," offered Burp apologetically. "Shall we forget about it this time, as long as she promises not to pretend to be a banshee again? What do you say?"

The girls' mouths hung open and by the look on old Thomas's face even Burp wished he hadn't just said that. But before Mr Thomas could answer there was a knock on the door; it was Miss Dennis. Burp and the girls were glad to see her smiling face and hoped that somehow she could save them.

"Sorry for barging in like this," she said in her soft, gentle voice. Her long, mousey-coloured hair was tied up in a bun revealing high cheek bones which looked almost fragile. The long blue dress she was wearing hid her small slim body. Burp had always had a secret crush on her, but he knew that she only saw him as a child.

Miss Dennis smiled sweetly and asked whether Wilf was in school today. Mr Thomas told her he was at the hospital because his mother had had an accident.

"Oh, dear!" she said, concern on her pretty face. "Is it ok if I take these three back to their class, then?"

"Good old Miss Dennis!" thought Burp, Molly and Kirsty, but their relief was short-lived.

"No, you cannot. I'll send them back when I've finished with them. Now will you kindly leave and attend to your class." Miss Dennis smiled and shrugged her shoulders at Burp and the girls as if to say, "Well, I tried". She walked to the door, but instead of opening it she locked it. "What on earth do you think you're doing?" demanded Mr Thomas.

135

Miss Dennis walked over to him, suddenly changed from a gentle woman to one showing arrogance and, without a word of warning, hit the Headmaster in the chest sending him flying back with such force that he slammed into the wall behind.

He stood propped up for a second, mouth hung open, eyes almost shut. Then he took a gasp of air and began to slide slowly down the wall, landing on the floor with his legs sticking out at angles, his head fallen forward and resting on his chest. Mr Thomas sat there motionless, making no sound, like a string puppet that had had its strings cut.

Miss Dennis turned to Burp, Molly and Kirsty.

"Don't even think of moving!" she snarled. The truth was, the three of them were too frightened to move. They knew that who - whatever - this thing was stood in front of them, it certainly wasn't Miss Dennis. A woman of her size could never have as much strength as she had just displayed; even the biggest and strongest of men could not release such force so easily.

Miss Dennis walked over to Mr Thomas and plucked him from the floor with just one hand, as though she had taken a pillow off the bed. He groaned as she lifted him.

"Thank God, he's alive!" gasped Molly.

"Please don't hurt him anymore, it's us you want," pleaded Kirsty. Burp couldn't speak; it had all happened so quickly. And Miss Dennis! She was the last person he would have thought of as being the banshee.

"I'll decide who to hurt!" she snarled with wild, staring eyes. Opening the top drawer of Mr Thomas's desk she pulled out a roll of thick parcel tape and, laying the Head's limp body on the desk, wound it round his arms and legs, finishing off by sticking a piece over his mouth; Mr Thomas looked like a half-wrapped mummy. Then, again picking up this huge man as if he was no weight at all, she carried him across the room and threw him into the store-cupboard.

Burp was praying that Liam would turn up as Miss Dennis told the three of them to look into her eyes. They did as they were told and Molly and Kirsty found that the more they looked, the more they wanted to look. Burp noticed that something was happening to the girls but strangely he wasn't affected. Then it hit him - it must be the Orf stone in his pocket.

"I'd better act the same way as the girls or I'll give the game away," he thought.

"It's no good trying to fight it. Enjoy being with me," whispered Miss Dennis in a low, soothing voice.

Burp saw that the girls' arms had dropped limply to their sides, their heads drooping slightly, eyes glazed and staring straight ahead as though they were sleeping with their eyes open. Burp thought they looked just like he did when he got up in the morning. He pretended to be entranced as well.

"Now follow me and don't look at any one," commanded Miss Dennis, taking the parcel tape with her as she walked out of the room. Burp was worried by all this, even more when he heard the comment Miss Dennis made as they walked along the corridor.

"It's time to show this miserable little world true power!" she said and let out a laugh that could have chilled a fireball.

Part Four

The Showdown

Mr Howe and Wilf arrived back at school and were pulling up the drive when they were greeted by the distraught figure of Miss Williams. She had a handkerchief held to her face and wasn't wearing any shoes. Mr Howe stopped the car and got out.

"Miss Williams! What on earth is wrong?" he asked, putting his arms round her for comfort.

"I'm leaving - I've just been assaulted!" she sobbed.

"Who has assaulted you?" asked a worried Mr Howe. Wilf could feel that something terrible was going to happen; he had a churning ache throughout his body. Miss Williams repeated the same thing over and over again.

"I've been assaulted!"

"Don't you think you should at least put your shoes back on?" asked Mr Howe.

"Keep them; I'm leaving!" sobbed Miss Williams.

Wilf didn't feel in the least bit sorry for her; he thought she was a hideous woman and had never liked her. He studied the woman: she was wearing her favourite coat which had at some stage of its existence been a beautiful animal.

"Ugliness wrapped in beauty is still ugly," thought Wilf. Miss Williams waddled off down the drive.

"I don't know what's happening, Wilf, but whatever it is, I don't like it!" said Mr Howe.

"Me neither, Sir," agreed Wilf.

"I think we'd better go and see Mr Thomas." They hurried to the Head's office and Mr Howe knocked on the door; no reply, so he knocked again and waited for the usual theatrical "ENTER" but it never came. Opening the door, Mr Howe looked in the room.

"That's strange, he's not in. I know he was going to be in his office all morning because that's why I took you to the hospital and not him. I'll just check his diary to see where he could be." They went into the office and as Mr Howe looked through the diary Wilf decided he could no longer keep up the lie about the crazy man; he knew he had to tell the truth but also realised that Mr Howe wouldn't believe him. Nevertheless, he was going to do it.

"Sir, I've got something to tell you," said Wilf, lowering his head in shame.

"What's that, then?" enquired Mr Howe. Wilf thought it better to explain why he lied first, hoping that would soften the blow.

"Sir, do you believe in the supernatural?"

"What do you mean? Like ghosts and ghouls?"

"Not exactly. More like pure evil."

"No, Wilf, I don't believe in pure evil. I think that every person, or beast, does what they see as their way. To them and others like them it is right, to others it is seen as wrong. Do you understand?"

"Not really, Sir, but getting back to the pure evil thing," said Wilf, thinking that he had just got off to a bad start, "do you think that there could be other worlds as well as ours?" Mr Howe looked at Wilf rather puzzled.

"On other planets, you mean?"

"I don't know, Sir. Maybe. Or do you think there could be lots of worlds that exist alongside our own?" Mr Howe started to laugh.

"I never had you down as a philosopher."

"I'm not, Sir, I don't even know what one is." Mr Howe knew that Wilf was trying to explain something and was about to ask him what was wrong when THUD came a loud noise from behind the store-cupboard door. Both jumped with fright.

"What the heck was that?" asked Mr Howe as he went towards the store-cupboard.

"Be careful, Sir, this could be what I've been trying to tell you about," said Wilf, backing away from the cupboard.

"Just what are you talking about?" asked Mr Howe, slowly reaching for the handle. THUD. There it was again, and again. They jumped back. Then Mr Howe took a deep breath and moved towards the door once more. Wilf's heart was racing like an express train - what if Mr Howe opened the door and the banshee came screaming out!

"Sir, I have to tell you that there's a large, black hairy beast in school out to kill me, Burp and possibly Molly and Kirsty!" shouted Wilf at the top of his voice as Mr Howe slowly turned the handle. Taking no notice he carried on while Wilf stood with his back against the wall, arms outstretched, waiting for something terrible to happen.

143

As the catch of the door was released Mr Howe felt a force push him from the other side, sending him sprawling backwards.

"Aargh!" he screamed with fright.

"Aargh!" screamed Wilf at Mr Howe's scream, jumping backwards with his hands over his face for protection, realising he was already against the wall and had nowhere to go. As the cupboard door was flung open out fell a trussed-up Mr Thomas who hit the floor like a sack of potatoes.

"Mr Thomas!" Wilf and Mr Howe gasped together. Mr Thomas was squirming on the floor like an over-fed caterpillar with his hair hung over his face like broken guitar strings. Wilf let out a sigh of relief - it wasn't the banshee! Then, as always, Wilf saw the funny side of it.

"I think we'd better call back later, Sir, Mr Thomas seems a bit tied up at the moment." Mr Thomas was desperately trying to say something. Mr Howe bent down and pulled the tape from his mouth.

"Ouch! I bet that hurt," winced Wilf as the tape pulled Mr Thomas's mouth so it looked like a monkey's.

"She has the children!" he gasped once the tape had been removed. Mr Howe started to remove the rest of the tape from around Mr Thomas's body as he struggled to free himself.

"Please calm down, Mr Thomas. Now tell me, who has what children and who did this to you?" The words "she's got the children" sent a chill through Wilf's heart.

"Where has she taken them?" pleaded Wilf.

"Do you know who did this, Wilf?" asked a puzzled Mr Howe.

144

"Yes, Sir - it's the banshee queen!" Wilf grabbed Mr Thomas with both hands and shook him. "Whose life-force is she using?"

"You must stop her; she has the children," repeated Mr Thomas, climbing to his feet.

"Will someone please tell me what the heck is happening here?" shouted Mr Howe.

"The banshee has Burp, Molly and Kirsty," explained Wilf.

"How did you know those were the children abducted?" asked Mr Thomas, coming round from his ordeal.

"I haven't got time to explain now. Just tell me who the banshee looks like."

"It wasn't a banshee, you stupid boy; it was Miss Deniss."

"Thank you," said Wilf. At least now he knew who to look for. He turned to Mr Howe. "Sir, you must trust me - only I can save them, but I need your help."

"No!" snapped Mr Howe. "Wilf - you can help me get the rest of the children out of school. Mr Thomas - you can 'phone the police. Now come on, Wilf, if Miss Deniss is still in school she could harm other children the state of mind that she's in." Wilf looked at Mr Howe.

"Why don't you listen to me? It's not Miss Deniss, it's the banshee!" he shouted before running out of the office.

Wilf could feel that the banshee was still around, but where? He ran to his class-room; maybe his classmates knew where Miss Deniss had gone. Mr Howe ran after Wilf.

"We must clear the school!" he shouted back to Mr Thomas, who nodded in agreement and 'phoned for the police.

145

Outside the office Mr Howe saw Wilf going into his class-room at the end of the corridor and gave chase. He found Wilf shouting at his class, urging them to tell him whether they had seen Miss Dennis, but the class ignored the boy. When Mr Howe walked in the children fell silent.

"Right, I want everyone to calmly go out to the playground. Now!" he ordered. "That means you as well, Wilf," he said, grabbing the lad by the arm. Just then the fire bell rang. "Good old Mr Thomas, that saves me from having to go round the school."

The rest of the children were asking if it was a real fire or just a practice. Mr Howe told them to do as they'd been asked. Wilf was struggling to break free from the teacher's grip.

"You don't understand! Only I can save them. They're my friends, and it's all my fault!" gasped Wilf as he tried to prize Mr Howe's fingers from his wrist.

"I do understand; they're your friends and you must be upset, but we must go outside and let the police deal with it." Mr Howe locked his arms around Wilf's chest and dragged him backwards, kicking and squirming to break free.

Outside, the playground was filling up with children, all asking the same question - what's wrong? Some were saying there was a real fire, others that it was a fire practice. Some even thought that a bomb had been planted in school. The teachers were telling the children to line up with their classmates. Mr Howe was still holding on to Wilf, knowing that if he let go of the lad he'd run off.

Then a scream rang out; it was one of the third year girls, pointing at the roof. Soon other children started to scream and shout and point. Mr Howe couldn't see properly from where he was stood so he moved forward, dragging Wilf with him. Finally, he saw what the children were pointing at which shocked him so much that he let go of Wilf.

"Oh, my God!" he gasped. Wilf was about to run off now that Mr Howe had let go when he too saw what everyone else had been looking at. He ran forward out of the crowd.

"No, please don't! It's me you want!" There, stood on the edge of the flat roof, was Miss Dennis, and from one outstretched arm hung Burp, dangling upside down by one leg. Miss Dennis saw Wilf in the playground below her.

147

"You! Wilf Sexton! You've got two minutes to get up here or I drop this brat. Come alone; if anyone else tries anything I've got another two brats up here that I'll drop!" she shouted, before letting out a blood-curdling laugh.

Wilf ran back into school, tears filling up in his eyes.

"Please don't hurt him! Please don't hurt him!" he sobbed, running up the first flight of stairs. Suddenly, he heard footsteps behind him.

"Liam!" he thought. "Thank God!" But as he turned to look he saw that it was Mr Howe. "Get back! You heard what she said; if anyone else turns up the banshee will drop Burp!" Wilf shouted at him.

"Wilf, for the last time, there is no such thing as a banshee. That's Miss Dennis up there who seems to have lost her senses." Wilf was now wiping the tears from his eyes; he knew that when he faced the banshee he mustn't show any fear.

"So little Miss Dennis is strong enough to hold Burp out at arms' length, as though he was a feather? And little Miss Dennis was strong enough to overpower Mr Thomas and tie him up when he's twice her size?" Mr Howe had to admit that Wilf did have a point.

"Well, I'm coming with you, then," he replied.

"If you come up with me you mustn't let her see you," said Wilf, then added, "Don't worry, help is on its way."

"I know, the police are here now."

"I'm not talking about the police, I'm talking about the most fearsome warrior you'll ever see. Just don't laugh at his skirt!"

Mr Howe didn't believe a word of this but had to

148

agree that if Wilf didn't get up to the roof soon, Miss Dennis might drop Burp.

They ran up two more flights before reaching the top. On the top staircase the roof ladders had been pulled down and as Wilf looked up through the manhole he could see the pale blue summer sky. He turned to Mr Howe.

"You must wait here." Mr Howe agreed and watched Wilf take a deep breath before climbing the ladder.

Once out on the roof he could feel the warm summer breeze, although it felt cooler than on the ground. To his right he could see a large water-tower held up by solid iron stilts; underneath were Molly and Kirsty, both with their hands and feet bound by the parcel tape that Miss Dennis had taken from Mr Thomas's office.

To his left he could see the back of Miss Dennis, still laughing at the screaming crowd below. She was tormenting them by shaking Burp as though he was a freshly-plucked chicken. Suddenly, she stopped laughing.

"So, you finally got here," she said without turning round. "I was just about to throw the brat to the crowd." She gave another laugh. "You know what I want - give me the stone!" she demanded, still holding Burp over the side.

"No!" he shouted back. Burp couldn't believe his ears.

"'No' is not good, Wilf!" shouted Burp, a quake in his voice. As he'd been swung upside down his t-shirt had fallen over his face and he was feeling sick as all the blood rushed to his head. "Why not try 'here's the stone, now can you please put my friend back onto the roof'?!" suggested Burp.

Wilf knew that he had a big problem here; the banshee wanted the stone but the banshee already had the stone because it was in Burp's pocket. If Wilf revealed this the beast might just take it then throw Burp over the side anyway. He had no choice but to try and bluff his way out. So, putting his hand into his pocket and pulling it back out in a fist, he tried to make it look as though he had the stone in his hand.

"Put Burp back onto the roof and I'll give you the stone," he shouted, then whispered, "I think now might be a good time to show, Liam." Looking around he was disappointed to see there was no sign of the warrior.

"You're in no position to bargain," shouted Miss Dennis.

"She's got a point, Wilf. Just give her the sto..." Burp stopped, suddenly realising he had it, and the same awful thought shot through his mind - she might take the stone and still throw him over the side. "Don't give her the stone!" he shouted, knowing full well that Wilf couldn't, even if he wanted to. Then Wilf had an idea.

"I'll smash the stone if you don't put Burp back onto the roof," he threatened.

"Good idea, Wilf!" agreed Burp.

"Then I'll throw you all off!" she replied.

"Bad idea!" decided Burp, scared that if he didn't get the right way up soon he would pass out.

Wilf moved to the edge of the roof with his fist still held out but keeping a distance between Miss Dennis and himself. He looked over the side to see the police getting everyone out of the playground while the marksmen got into position.

Since Wilf could now talk to Miss Dennis without shouting he hoped this might calm down the situation.

150

"If I smash the stone you'll never get back to your own world, you'll be stuck here. Do you see those men dressed in blue down there? They're *our* warriors. If you drop Burp they'll shoot you, not with a bow and arrow, but with a gun," said Wilf as calmly as he could.

"What is a gun?" asked Miss Dennis.

"It's something you can't argue with, so put me back on the roof!" screamed Burp.

"My friend's right," agreed Wilf. "The gun fires a bullet that can pass through your body from over a mile away." Miss Dennis thought for a second.

"If I give you the brat, you must then place the Orf stone down and say you hand your powers to me."

"Whatever you say." Miss Dennis pulled Burp up as though he was a paper-weight and moved away from the edge, dragging the boy's head on the floor.

"You have to let him go," said Wilf. Miss Dennis looked at the boy, then releasing her grip let Burp fall onto the roof. He tried to jump to his feet but was so dizzy that he fell over and had to scramble away instead.

"Now, the stone!" snapped Miss Dennis. Wilf knew that once the beast had the stone it would be invincible and would probably kill them all.

Out of the corner of his eye he could see Burp, removing the sticky tape from Molly and Kirsty, and knew they needed time to escape. He also knew that if Liam didn't come soon, and the banshee found out he didn't have the stone, he himself would almost certainly be killed.

"You promise that we can all go free once you have the stone?" asked Wilf, playing for time.

151

"No more bargaining. Give me the stone or I'll kill you all!" shouted Miss Dennis.

Wilf knew that this was it - he could stall no more. Shaking with fear he slowly placed his fist to the ground. He shut his eyes. In his mind he was pleading for Liam to turn up. Out of ideas, all Wilf could think was that he would open his fist, then scream for Molly, Kirsty and Burp to run. At least that way the stone would be safe, and so would each world.

Opening his eyes and glancing across at Burp he saw that the girls were untied. He took a deep breath.

"It's now or never!" he thought, but before he had chance to say anything there was a brilliant flash of light and a loud BOOM! Miss Dennis was sent flying backwards with such force that it looked as though she'd been hit by a cannon-ball.

"Liam!" shouted Wilf. "Am I glad to see y..." Wilf stopped in mid sentence. "No... it can't be!" he gasped. Standing in front of him was not Liam but a large, black beast with steaming matted hair all over its body, murderous blood-red eyes staring straight at him. "No!" he gasped again. "It can't be! I was told there was just one banshee." It moved closer; Wilf backed off. The banshee opened its mouth to reveal large, pointed, blood-stained teeth.

"Surprise, surprise!" the banshee hissed in a low, rasping tone. "You are right, my friend. In this world there is only one banshee; that is me."

"So who's that, then?" asked Wilf, nervously pointing to the limp body of Miss Dennis sprawled out on the roof.

"I will show you." The banshee walked over to her. Wilf could hear the large, sharp claws on the beast's feet sticking into the felt roof. It kicked Miss Dennis; her body doubled-up with pain. "I waited for the life force to get weak before I made my move. He's been in that life form too long and no longer has any strength."

Burp, Molly and Kirsty ran to Wilf's side; they were

going to face this together.

"Did you say 'he'?" asked Burp.

"Look and see for yourselves." The banshee pointed its long, clawed finger at Miss Dennis and as they watched the body started to glow, so brightly that they had to cover their eyes. Eventually the light faded leaving not Miss Dennis sprawled out on the roof but – LIAM! The four of them gasped.

"It can't be!" Wilf was stunned.

"I knew there was something strange about him," said Burp.

"Who is it?" asked Molly and Kirsty together.

"That's who I've been waiting for to come and save us for the last quarter of an hour," replied Wilf.

"It's Liam, the man in the skirt that we told you about," explained Burp.

Liam was trying to pull himself up but they could see that he was very weak.

"You said he was on our side," said Kirsty.

"Yeah, that's what he told us," replied Burp.

"He's gorgeous!" said Molly wistfully, looking at Liam's powerful body. Wilf was hurt by Molly's remark.

"How can you say that about a bloke who wears a skirt?"

The banshee let out a low, hissing laugh that sounded like gas escaping from a pipe in short bursts. The four friends fell silent when they realised they were still in great danger.

The banshee bent down and ripped away the small bag of herbs that Liam had tied to his belt, staring at him menacingly.

"We don't want you taking anything that could make

you better, do we now?" It threw the bag off the roof.

"So, what happens now? I suppose you've come to kill us all," reasoned Wilf. The banshee moved closer and he couldn't help but look into its murderous red eyes.

"What has the big monkey-man been telling you?" the banshee asked Wilf, who couldn't help but notice how the beast had become so much less threatening. However, he still had no intention of trusting it, not after what had happened with Liam. He was one of his own kind and look what he'd done!

Suddenly, Wilf had a thought. If he could get the banshee to the edge of the roof the police would surely shoot it. So he moved closer to the edge hoping that the banshee would follow, giving the police marksmen a clear shot.

Mr Howe, meanwhile, was climbing the ladders leading to the roof, expecting to catch Miss Dennis by surprise.

Wilf kept talking to the banshee.

"Liam's told us how you stole the cauldron of life and tried to destroy his world," he said, still trying to move closer to the edge of the roof. The banshee let out a loud piercing howl of a laugh that echoed through the wind, forcing everyone to cover their ears in pain. The four of them cowered away from the beast.

"It was not us who stole the cauldron of life, but him and his monkey warriors!" rasped the banshee.

Molly moved forward; she looked so tiny stood next to this huge beast but knew that if they were all to get out of this alive the best way would be to talk. After all, they had no chance in a fight.

"Then why don't you tell us what happened. And why

155

do you keep calling Liam a monkey when he's not?" she said, her head held high. The banshee looked down at Molly - and smiled! They were shocked.

"You are a very bright child, and very brave. You must be female," said the banshee in a low, almost kind, voice.

"Of course I'm female!" she snapped, upset that the banshee couldn't tell she was a girl. The banshee realised the girl had been offended.

"I'm sorry, but all you monkeys look the same to me."

"Will you stop calling us monkeys! We are human beings," replied Molly.

The banshee let out another high-pitched wail, forcing them all to cover their ears again. Molly suddenly realised that this noise was not a threat, but a laugh. The banshee was actually laughing! But it has to be said it was the scariest laugh she'd ever heard.

The beast bent down and gently held out its huge, clawed hand.

"Come child, take my hand." Molly gulped when she saw the huge, sharp, white talons on the end of the long, powerful fingers but was surprised how soft the palm of the banshee's hand looked; it was black and shiny, just like satin. "Don't be frightened, child, I will not hurt you."

Molly believed she was not in danger; if the banshee was as evil as they had been told it would have killed them all by now.

She placed her small, white hand on the huge palm of the banshee's and smiled.

"No, Molly! Don't!" shouted Wilf, afraid for her safety.

"It's ok," replied Molly as she felt the banshee's warm,

soft hand close around hers and give a gentle squeeze of reassurance.

"Let me explain," said the banshee, beckoning the others closer. "I call your kind monkeys because you were all once monkey-like creatures; some of you still act the same as the monkeys that swing in the trees. But I know that it's unfair to class you all together, so for that I apologise. I know that to you I must look frightening, but you must realise that to my children *he* looks just as frightening," said the banshee pointing to Liam, still lying on the floor unable to move.

Kirsty moved closer to the banshee. Burp hesitated for a second or two but then joined her.

"What are you all doing? You're being fooled!" shouted Wilf, still at the edge of the roof. The banshee turned to him.

"Your friends want to reason, unlike you who just want me to go to the edge so the people below can kill me." Wilf was shocked that the banshee had worked out his plan but still didn't trust it and stayed where he was.

Mr Howe had reached the doorway to the roof and was wondering how to overpower Miss Dennis, unaware there had been quite a few changes since Wilf had left him. He could see the shadows of Burp, Molly and Kirsty from his position but couldn't understand what the unusually-large shadow was.

He took a deep breath and jumped out onto the roof, hoping to overpower Miss Dennis, but the sight that greeted him scared him so much that he froze to the spot. His mouth hung open, and if he had opened his eyes any wider his eyeballs would have dropped out. He pointed at the banshee and started to make a strange babbling sound.

"Bu... bu... bu..."

"Sir, close your mouth, you sound like a motor boat," said Molly.

"It's ok, Sir, it won't hurt you," added Kirsty. The banshee glared at Mr Howe and its eyes lit up as though on fire. Still in a state of shock, the teacher was unable to move.

"Don't be afraid, Sir. Remember, there's no such thing as banshees!" Wilf called out from the edge of the roof.

The banshee spoke to Mr Howe in a low, calm voice.

"Please do not try to attack me or I will have to defend myself. I do not wish to harm any of you."

"Sir, you must listen to what it has to say," added Molly. Mr Howe stared in disbelief.

"Now I must explain the truth. We haven't much time before the warrior regains his strength," said the beast, before explaining what had happened in its own world.

"The marsh warriors were set up to stop wars in their world, wars which had lasted for hundreds of years. Once they had all joined together they swore never to fight against each other again, bringing about peace and great prosperity.

"But as time went on there seemed less and less reason to have marsh warriors and the people began to dislike their arrogance and power. In return, the warriors thought that the people they were there to save had no respect for them. The warrior leader knew that to regain this respect he had to make the people need him, and the only way for this to happen would be if there was a war.

"So, unable to fight against each other, they needed a new enemy, one so frightening that the people would beg for the warriors' help."

"You mean like banshees?" asked Wilf, who had now moved away from the edge of the roof. The banshee let out its low, hissing laugh again.

"You sound interested," said the banshee, its huge red tongue curled in its mouth as it spoke.

"Let's just say that it's all starting to make sense." The

159

banshee smiled to reassure him, then continued the story.

"The banshees were the guardians of the cauldron of life which has in it the power that keeps worlds alive and apart. Many people have heard about it, but most thought it to be a myth. That was how we wanted to keep it, until one day the marsh warriors found a way into our world, we don't know how.

"The day they arrived could not have been better for them because the cauldron was being moved, something which happened quite regularly; if left in one place for too long it would encase itself in rock, never to be found again.

"Since we thought that no one knew the existence of our world, only a few of my most trusted people were moving the cauldron; I now realise that I was foolish not to have more guards for something so important.

"To cut a long story short, my people were overpowered and killed and the cauldron stolen. We had no choice but to try and get it back. As the banshee queen I was the only one allowed to drink from the cauldron, so using my life-force I took a small band of my best warriors and entered his world." The banshee pointed at Liam, still motionless.

"Liam told us about the fight for the cauldron didn't he, Wilf? He told us how the warrior had placed his hand into the cauldron for power, and how he was scarred by the banshee," said Burp.

The banshee let go of Molly's hand and walked over to Liam. Then, with its huge talons, ripped his tunic from his body with one swipe.

The lads gasped; there was a huge scar running diagonally across his chest.

160

"Like this one?" asked the banshee.

"You mean Liam was the leader of the marsh warriors?" asked Wilf. The banshee nodded its head.

"So that's why he got so excited when he was telling us the story; he was reliving what had happened!" added Burp.

The banshee walked back to the children. Mr Howe had moved forward, still quiet, still staring in disbelief.

"His plan worked so well," explained the banshee. "When I arrived in their world with my small band of warriors his people were terrified and tried to attack us. We tried to reason but they wouldn't listen. A banshee will not fight unless it is attacked; we had no option but to defend ourselves and I am sad to say that we hurt many of his people.

"The marsh warriors were then called upon, becoming heroes once more. We were but a small force and could not take on great battles with the powerful marsh warriors so were forced to hide and search in secret for the cauldron. This was seen as a great victory for the marsh warriors, who were given more power in their world than they had ever imagined.

"But like most beings with too much power it wasn't long before the big monkey-man started to abuse it, and soon his people lived in terror - not from us, the banshees, but from him, the great saviour.

"Once his people had had enough they were more than willing to listen to what I had to say as they were now no more than his slaves. I promised them that if they helped me to find the cauldron I would then have the power to bring my army to their world, defeat him, and take the cauldron and my army back to my own world.

"It wasn't long before some of his own warriors had

161

had enough; they saw themselves as honourable defenders, not enslavers.

"One of the warriors deciding to help us was a close aid to the big monkey-man and knew where the cauldron was hidden. This was the turning point; soon we were able to recapture the cauldron easily as there were only a few men guarding it, the monkey-man fearing that too many guardians might lead to the discovery of the source of his power."

The banshee was so busy telling what had happened and the rest were so busy listening that nobody had noticed the police marksmen who had lined up to take a shot.

They couldn't believe what they were looking at. Through their gun sights they could see the figures of Mr Howe and the four children and in front of them, towering head and shoulders above, was the huge, frightening figure of the banshee.

Some of the marksmen rubbed their eyes in disbelief and radioed back telling of a strange beast, asking what they should do. The message came through to shoot at the first chance they got, so they focused on the banshee; how could they miss something so huge!

One of the marksmen was on the school roof on the opposite side and it was decided he had the best shot. Lining the banshee up in his sights he slowly gripped the trigger of the gun.

"Perfect - right between the eyes!" he thought. Holding his breath, he started to squeeze the trigger.

"Can I hold your hand again?" Molly asked the banshee. All her fear had now disappeared, believing what the banshee said to be true.

"Certainly, my dear," it replied, gently holding out its huge, clawed hand.

"Oh, no! It's going to kill the child!" thought the marksman, firing.

In the blink of an eye the bullet hit its target, not between the eyes as the banshee had moved to hold Molly's hand, but in the side of the neck.

The beast fell backwards, howling with pain, the noise louder than a hundred fire sirens, while the others dived to the floor. Blood was spurting from the banshee's neck, its huge hand covering the wound to try and stem the flow. Molly jumped to her feet.

"Stop! Stop!" she cried, waving her arms in the air and facing the marksman. The rest of the group crowded round the banshee so no more shots could be fired.

The beast tried to speak, making an eerie, gurgling noise as blood seeped from its mouth and trickled down its jaw.

"Please don't die!" sobbed Molly.

The rest had tears in their eyes; the beast they had once feared so much had turned out to be a gentle giant who had saved their lives. Now all they could do was stand and watch as the life slowly drained from its body.

Molly took hold of the banshee's hand. With tears streaming down her face she gently put her head on the huge, hairy chest.

"You were right; we are just monkeys, we kill what we fear, and we fear what is different," sobbed the girl.

With its last breath the banshee looked at Wilf, its eyes barely open, those same eyes that had once sent a chill

163

through his body. Slowly they were closing, and Wilf just wanted them to open again.

The banshee beckond him to its side and spoke in a low, gurgling voice.

"You are the stone master, do..." Stopping for a moment to swallow the blood in its throat the beast continued, by now too weak to open its eyes. "Do not let the big monkey get the stone." Gently, it stroked Molly's head. "Look after him, he... he will need your wisdom." With that the banshee fell silent - and lifeless.

"Give me the stone!" boomed a loud voice from behind. They all jumped with fright and had every reason to be afraid because there stood Liam, sword and shield in hand. He smiled.

"I was waiting to get a shot at it but it looks like your people beat me to it."

"That's the first time I've seen you smile," said a tearful Burp. "It seems that only death makes you happy."

"It isn't dead - you can't kill it!" answered Liam.

"She's not an 'it', she's a person!" snapped Kirsty.

Suddenly, Mr Howe jumped to his feet.

"Leave these children alone!" he shouted, placing himself between them and the warrior. Liam gave Mr Howe a cold stare, full of hate.

"Move - or die!" he growled. Mr Howe put his arms behind his back in an attempt to shield the youngsters. Then, without warning, Liam kicked out and hit Mr Howe in the stomach sending him flying into the air, doubled-up. The teacher landed several feet away in a heap, clutching his stomach and trying to get his breath back. Liam walked to him, sword held high.

"Leave him alone!" screamed Kirsty, grabbing the hand holding the weapon. Then the warrior did something which shocked the others so much they were unable to move. As Kirsty grabbed Liam's hand he shrugged her off with ease and hit her with the hilt of his sword. There was a sickening crack as it connected with the girl's fragile cheek and her body was sent flying, hitting the iron stilts holding up the water tower. She lay there, lifeless.

Liam moved towards Mr Howe, desperately trying to get to his feet, as though nothing had happened and showed no mercy, bringing his razor-sharp sword slamming down onto his victim's back. Wilf felt sick at the sound of the dull thud the sword made as it struck home. Burp and Molly winced and looked away but Wilf couldn't take his eyes off Mr Howe, motionless on the floor.

The marksmen had started to move in but were stopped by a new call: ANOTHER TARGET ON THE ROOF. They took up their positions again. Liam knew he might have the same fate as the banshee so grabbed Molly to use as a shield, knowing the police wouldn't fire as long as he had hold of her. He was right; another call went out to the maksmen: THE TARGET HAS A HOSTAGE, HOLD YOUR FIRE. REPEAT, HOLD YOUR FIRE.

Molly looked so small as she wriggled to break free from Liams grip, but he held her tightly to his chest. Wilf and Burp could see that Molly couldn't breathe as Liam's powerful arms slowly squeezed tighter and tighter round her waist, like a python killing its prey.

"Give me the stone!" commanded Liam again. Wilf

and Burp stood with tears streaming down their faces. Both felt so helpless and confused; they had no one to turn to and knew Liam would stop at nothing to get the stone. Wilf took a deep breath just to stop himself from crying. He had no option but to give Liam the stone; he had lost, Liam had won.

"Let Molly go and you can have the stone!" he shouted, trying not to look Liam in the eye. The warrior sneered at Wilf with contempt.

"You are in no position to bargain," he mocked.

Molly's body had become limp and she was hanging over Liam's arm like an overcoat. Burp had run over to where Kirsty lay motionless and was bent down stroking her hair, now soaked in blood.

"Kirsty, I'm so sorry!" he sobbed, gently taking her hand and kissing it. "You were so brave, and I was such a coward!" he whispered as he looked at her face, unreconisable because of her injury. Wilf watched his friend and understood his pain.

"Why?" he asked. "Why did you have to do all this for the stone? Why didn't you just take it off me in the Castle of Endless Time? Or when we were on the moors?" Liam laughed.

"I wasn't with you in the Castle of Endless Time. That was the wolf. What I told you about the banshee and the warrior being one was true. When I drank from the cauldron I took on its life-force and we both had to be locked away for the safety of worlds, so they said. The wolf agreed; all it cares about are the worlds. All that power going to waste."

"But all the banshee wanted was peace."

"Oh, very noble, but it's a beast. Just look at it! How could my people listen to such a creature?"

167

"She may look like a beast but she was gentle and loving whereas you are just a beast," snapped Wilf. Liam laughed again.

"When you came to the Castle of Endless Time I tried to get the stone from you then. It was I, not the wolf, who took the form of your mother. When I realised that the wolf had taken on my appearance I had no choice but to try and scare you into giving me the stone."

"So it was the banshee on the moors with us then?"

"No, that was me, but I needed the wolf to be near when I took the stone; because it has been charged by the cauldron the stone is the only thing that can kill the wolf and set me free."

"So that's why you wanted me to bring some friends; you were going to use them to lure the banshee into a trap. You planned to kill us all along, didn't you?"

"What are a few useless lives when I could unite worlds?!"

"You mean rule worlds and enslave the people."

While the two were talking, Burp had taken off his t-shirt and placed it under Kirsty's head. As he looked at her he felt a powerful anger build up inside and, standing up, walked over to Liam, fists clenched, wanting to fight.

"Life means nothing to you, does it? Well, let me tell you that we're not useless. In fact, you need Wilf."

"Burp, leave it! Walk away; he'll only kill you as well!" shouted Wilf to his friend. Burp put his hand into his pocket and pulled out the Orf stone, holding it up to Liam.

"Look! I've got the stone. All that time you had hold of me, you already had it. You're not so clever!" Liam let out a scream of anger and lunged at Burp. Molly swung round like a little rag doll in his arms as he moved. Burp jumped back and threw the stone.

"Catch, Wilf!" Wilf jumped into the air with his hands cupped and caught the stone. "Wilf is the stone master. You need him, he has the power!" teased Burp, making a run for the stairs and safety. Liam followed, determined not to let him escape.

"NO!" screamed Wilf, holding out the Orf stone. "I command you to stop!" he shouted, hoping that this would stop Liam; it didn't.

As Burp ran, one of the laces on his trainers, which he never fastened, got caught under his foot sending him flying. Liam came running up.

"Arrgghh!" screamed the warrior. Sword in one hand, Molly in the other, he grabbed Burp by the neck and wrenched him into the air, throwing him across the roof like a discus. Burp bounced once on the roof before hitting the edge and scrabbled as he felt his body going over the side, unable to get a grip on the roof felt.

Wilf, watching in horror, ran to catch hold of his friend before he plummeted to the ground far below. Burp looked up, his face full of fear, and held out his hand. Wilf dived but missed Burp's fingertips by millimetres and could only watch in horror as he rolled over the edge, as though in slow motion.

"No!!" screamed Wilf as he heard the sickening sound of Burp's body thud onto the concrete below. Looking over the edge he could see his body on the playground, arms and legs twisted into unnatural positions. From the side of his head

170

blood was starting to trickle out onto the floor.

Wilf could take no more and burst into tears; all his friends were now dead. He looked around the roof at the carnage that had occurred in such a short space of time: there was the banshee which had tried to save them - although Liam said it wasn't dead it lay there lifeless, a gun shot wound to the neck; Mr Howe, the teacher he had most respected, killed by Liam's sword; Kirsty - although he hadn't got to know her too well, he knew that she was a special kind of person; and Molly, sweet Molly, brave and beautiful, the girl he had always secretly fancied, was being used as a human shield, the life squeezed out of her.

Wilf looked over the edge again at Burp and could see police and paramedics crowding round his lifeless body. This was his best friend, the person who knew all his secrets, the one who always stood by him no matter what and was like a brother. Wilf put his head in his hands and sobbed.

"It's all my fault! They all died because of me. Oh, why did I ever swallow that stupid stone in the first place?"

Liam approached.

"It's over!" he sneered. "Hand me the stone and say that you pass the powers of the stone master to me." Wilf looked at him through his fingers that were covering his face. On the outside Liam looked just like you would expect a Celtic hero to: tall, strong, handsome, but on the inside he was bitter, selfish and murderous.

Wilf pulled his hands away from his face; he still had the Orf stone in his hand. He looked at the stone; he didn't want it. Such a small piece of stone had caused the deaths of nearly all the people he cared about. How could he go on,

171

knowing that all these people were dead because of him? What would he do without Burp?

"Give me the stone!" shouted Liam, his voice full of anger and impatience. Wilf glared at him.

"What a hideous creature!" he thought, tears still streaming down his face. Suddenly, Wilf felt an explosion of anger. "You will never, ever get this stone. It causes nothing but misery for people. I wish I'd never seen it. I wish I'd never made all those stupid wishes!" snapped Wilf. Then it hit him like a bolt of lightning. "Of course, that's it! Why didn't I think of it before!" he shouted, jumping about laughing.

"Give me the stone. Now! I don't have time for this childishness!" shouted Liam. Wilf was now too excited to care about him.

"What are you going to do if I don't give you the stone? You can't kill me until I hand the powers over to you. Anyway, you won't need the stone where you're going!" Liam looked confused.

"What are you talking about, child?" he shouted. Wilf stopped jumping around and held up the Orf stone between his thumb and fore finger so that Liam could see.

"I'm talking about this. Would you like to see a magic trick?" asked Wilf, calmly and confidently. Liam just glared back at Wilf, knowing that what he'd said was true. The boy continued. "You're going to like this trick. Not a lot!" he said, waving the Orf stone at Liam. "Now you see it, now you don't!" With that Wilf popped the stone into his mouth and swallowed. Liam couldn't believe it.

"NO!" he screamed, throwing Molly's body to one side. As he did so there was a crack of gun-fire. Liam fell back as though he'd just been hit by an invisible punch. Wilf ran over to the warrior, now on his knees holding his chest, blood seeping through his fingers. He looked at Wilf with wild, staring eyes, his mouth hung open but unable to speak.

"I want you to hear this before you go," growled Wilf, pushing his face into Liam's. "I wish that it was yesterday again and I hadn't swallowed the stone."

Wilf knew that by swallowing the stone he could make wishes again and that this wish would stop everything; Liam and the banshee would be back in the Castle of Endless Time, Molly, Kirsty, Burp and Mr Howe would all be alive again and just as a bonus Wilf himself wouldn't remember a thing about this nightmare ordeal.

It wasn't long before Wilf felt the strange buzzing feeling in his stomach and soon things began to look blurred. He could just make out Liam's face.

"Goodbye!" he said, then punched Liam on the end of his nose.

"Come along, children, we must move on," said Miss Dennis, the teacher of class six. All the children moved on except two, Wilf Sexton and Burp Dawson. They were standing in front of a table covered with a green baize cloth, seeing who could pull the most disgusting face. Burp was winning.

Neither knew what had happened. Once again they were just two ordinary lads messing about instead of learning. Everything was as it was and how it should be. The banshee and Liam were back in the Castle of Endless Time and the lads didn't even know that they existed. Molly, Kirsty, Burp and Mr Howe were all alive and well.

Wilf walked over to the table covered with green baize and looked at the sign that said "PLEASE DO NOT TOUCH THE EXHIBITS" then leaned over and picked up a little stone object.

"I mean, what the heck is this supposed to be?" asked Wilf, holding it between his thumb and fore finger.

"It looks like an old baked bean to me," replied Burp.

"I can't believe we've travelled all the way from Huddersfield to Manchester just to see an old baked bean!"

said Wilf, shaking his head.

"Ah, but is it a tasty baked bean asked Burp?"

"I don't know, young man. I'll have a taste and tell you," said Wilf, popping the stone into his mouth.

"What on earth are you two doing here...?"

The "Thank you, Luvvies"

Thanks to Steve Rudd and Terry Sorfleet. Also to Debbie Nunn for editing this book so people can actually read my rantings. (My ritting is geting betterr, Deb!) Thanks to Julie Thompson for her brilliant illustrations and for just smiling when I kept ranting on about how the banshee needed to be more scary. Also to Phil Rendell, who I know will sell thousands of copies of this book for me.

Thanks to Carol and Lee for listening to me drivel on about how I think this story works. And, last but not least, thanks to Mr Howe, my old English teacher, for letting me use him in this book. (I recently met him again after twenty years while on a bus journey; I think he thought it was a mugging when I accosted him!)